three torrid tales of triple passion
from New York Times Bestselling Author
Opal Carew.

THREE

Three brothers. Three happy endings.
Let the journey begin.

Hot steamy dreams... a sexy stranger...
and his two brothers...
all add up to an erotic adventure she'll never forget.

THREE MEN AND A BRIDE

Now that you've read Lori and Craig's story, maybe you'd
like to go back and learn more about Marie and Drake in this
prequel to Three.

What do you do when you can't stop lusting after your new
husband's two gorgeous brothers?

THREE SECRETS

Now are you ready for Abel's happy ending?

Keeping one secret is intriguing. Two is naughty. Three...deserves to
be punished.
Sharing secrets has never been so exhilarating...

THREE HAPPY ENDINGS

OPAL CAREW

To Laurie,
I couldn't have done it without you.

CONTENTS

THREE

Three brothers. Three happy endings.
Let the journey begin.

Hot steamy dreams... a sexy stranger...
and his two brothers...
all add up to an erotic adventure she'll never forget.

CHAPTER 1

Lori clung to his shoulders, reveling in the heat of his muscular body pressed tight against her. His glittering blue eyes locked with hers and he smiled.

Oh, God. She didn't even know his name.

She shivered as he positioned his huge erection against her damp opening. Then he pushed forward. She gasped at his intimate invasion. *So long.*

She had waited so long.

He drew back, then glided forward again, filling her deeply. Joy bubbled within her. Her heart pumped, propelling hot blood through her veins, accelerating her intense desire. Adrenaline coursed through her as he pumped forward and back. Forward and back. Explosive energy built inside her and she gasped for air. She could feel it starting. What she'd been longing for. Very soon she would experience the orgasm of a lifetime.

He glided into her, again and again, heightening the pleasure. Anticipation quivered through her. Building…building—

A loud buzzing grated in her ear. The feel of his hard cock faded away to an empty ache as she opened her eyes.

Oh, damn. It had been only a dream.

She slammed her hand on the alarm clock to shut it up and dragged herself from the bed. She had to do something. She'd been obsessing about this sexy stranger for three months now.

He was the most incredibly attractive man she'd ever seen. Tall, broad-shouldered with blue eyes that twinkled when he smiled. And, man, he had a killer smile. Just the thought of it made her wet.

She groaned as she climbed into the shower. She'd only seen him across a crowded subway station at rush hour, yet she still remembered his strong, square jaw, his wavy dark hair with an errant curl that he absently pushed from his forehead... and his full, sexy lips.

She thought of those lips kissing her as she soaped her breasts, tweaking the nipples until they stood erect, then she lathered between her legs. The water sluiced over her body, rinsing the soap away, as she pictured the sexy stranger standing in front of her. She shoved her fingers inside her vagina, imagining him pushing his cock into her.

Oh, yeah. She had it bad. She thrust her fingers in and out, moving faster and faster as her other hand traveled back to her nipple to finger it mercilessly.

She could imagine *his* hand tweaking her nipple, *his cock* moving inside her. She moved her thumb to flick her clit. The heat built to an incredible height, until she felt she would spontaneously combust, then her vaginal muscles clamped around her fingers as she climaxed.

She finished her shower and toweled off. She pulled on her terry robe then padded into her den and flicked on the computer screen to check her email.

She'd actually caught sight of him one other time, about

three weeks later, leaving the travel agent in the mall above her subway stop, but he hadn't noticed her and he'd disappeared down the escalator and into the crowd of commuters before she could catch up to him. Not that she knew what she would have said to him.

Hi, there. I've been dreaming about you for weeks. Let's slip away and have a quick tumble.

There were twelve unread messages in her inbox, but she clicked directly on the third one, from Marie, her best friend who was currently on a singles tour in Costa Rica. She'd asked Lori to join her, but even if she hadn't been going totally crazy from long hours at work, Lori didn't have the money for a trip like that.

Okay, I know you're going to think I'm totally crazy but...

I'm getting married!!! :-)

I met him on the plane – we're both on the same singles tour. His name is Drake.

We're doing it here. You know how complicated it would get if I had a big wedding at home -- with the way Dad and Mom go at each other anytime they're in the same room, and add her new boyfriend to the mix and... well, it would be a total disaster. Anyway, who can argue with getting married by a gorgeous waterfall in sunny Costa Rica?

The wedding is on Saturday, then we're flying home Sunday.

If you could fly down, that would be great, but I understand if you can't...

The email went on a little longer, but the words blurred in front of Lori's eyes as she noticed the photo at the bottom of the message.

It couldn't be.

She clicked on it to enlarge and...

Oh, my God. It's him.

CHAPTER 2

How would Lori possibly get through the weekend with Marie and her new husband, Drake, the man who still starred in her erotic dreams?

After Lori had turned down two invitations to dinner and a couple more for drinks, always claiming work issues, Marie had finally insisted Lori give her a date when she could join them at Drake's family cottage near Lake Simcoe, north of Toronto.

She hadn't wanted to drive up with them, in case she came up with a brilliant plan to cut the weekend short without hurting Marie's feelings.

She tucked the bouquet of fresh cut flowers under her arm and clung to the strap of her small suitcase as she rang the doorbell. The place was huge. It was more like a full-fledged home than what Lori thought of as a cottage.

Marie opened the door and squealed, then pulled Lori inside and threw her arms around her, practically knocking the flowers flying.

Marie pulled back and grinned at Lori, then held out her left hand and wiggled her fingers. A bright, shiny diamond glittered on her ring finger. Lori grasped Marie's hand and stared admiringly.

"It's gorgeous."

And it was. A marquis cut solitaire in a white gold setting. The matching band had a delicate pattern engraved on the surface.

"Here, I brought some flowers." Lori handed Marie the bouquet.

"Lovely. Thanks." She led Lori into a large, gourmet kitchen and grabbed a crystal vase from the cupboard beside the stainless steel, double door refrigerator, then filled the vase with water.

Lori peeled the paper from the flowers and placed them in the vase.

"Perfect." Marie's face glowed.

Well, why not? She was a brand new bride and she seemed very happy. "Come on. Let me show you around."

"Where's... ah... Drake," Lori asked.

"Oh, he won't be arriving until late tonight." Marie grinned. "He thought you and I would like some girl time to catch up without the new husband getting in the way." She waved a dismissive hand. "I told him there'd be no problem but... he seemed almost nervous to meet you. Imagine that."

Nervous? So, did that mean he'd recognized her, too? Did he have feelings of lust in return? The mere possibility sent Lori's hormones dancing, chased away by guilt... and the realization that if it were true, the weekend would be excruciatingly long and awkward.

Sunshine danced along the polished, dark hardwood floors as Lori padded into the kitchen, awakened by the smell of coffee. The house was very quiet. Marie and Drake must still be asleep. The coffee maker had probably been set to automatic.

She slipped into the kitchen, poured herself a cup and carried it to the stools that sat in front of the counter, facing a fabulous view of the lake. As she took a seat, she noticed a note on the black granite counter top.

'Gone to do some grocery shopping. Back about one.'

Lori glanced at the clock. It was only nine now. That meant she had the house to herself for four hours.

She ate a quick breakfast then pulled on her bikini and headed for the patio doors to the backyard. She stepped through to a paradise of plants, stone decking, and a gorgeous free form pool with a waterfall—and even a hot tub.

Wow, her idea of heaven.

She stretched out on one of the lounge chairs and opened her book. After about a half hour, she dropped her book onto the table beside the chair and rolled onto her stomach. She undid the strap of her top to maximize her tan and tucked her hands under her head. The sun beat down on her, lulling her into a quiet nap.

"You're going to burn if you're not careful."

A man's voice—it must be Drake's—startled her. She flushed as she realized from the back, with her thong bottoms and her top strap undone, she might as well be naked.

"You need some protection."

She saw his masculine hands pick up her tube of sun block from the table beside her and felt the warm lotion form a line across her back. His large hand stroked her flesh as he massaged it in: first across her shoulders, then down her back, then the length of each leg. Next, she felt his hand cup one of her ass cheeks as he slowly and thoroughly massaged the lotion into her skin. She longed to flip over and allow him to give the same attention to other parts of her body. Her breasts tingled and her vagina tightened with need.

But he was just being a good host. He didn't want her to sunburn. She couldn't stand the wonderful feel of his hands caressing her a moment longer. It felt too good. She clutched her bathing suit top to her chest and rolled over to a sitting position.

"Thanks, Drake, I think I'm well covered now."

He smiled that electric smile of his and winked. "Whatever you say."

He stood up and she nearly gasped. He wore the briefest, sexiest bathing suit she'd ever seen on a man. It left little to the imagination. She could see the length of his cock straining against the thin fabric, the head nearly pushing out the top. Clearly, applying the sun block had affected him just as much as it had affected her.

If Marie were to step out on the deck right now, it would be very embarrassing.

"Where... uh... where is Marie?"

"She went out shopping. Didn't you see her note?"

Alone. They were alone? Panic shot through her. He was practically naked in front of her, and obviously turned on. A little voice inside her suggested she drop her hands to her sides and let her top fall to the ground. That would certainly heat things up between them.

But she couldn't. This was her best friend's husband.

"By the way, I'm not Drake." He sat on the lounge chair facing her.

"What?" She stared at him, perplexed.

"I'm Drake's brother, Craig." At her narrowing eyes, he continued, "I'm not kidding."

"You're identical—"

"That's right. Marie said she was having a friend visit this weekend and thought I'd like to meet you. I'm glad I took her up on the invitation." His gaze shifted up and down her body, coming to rest on her breasts, and her hands clinging to the loose bikini top.

"Nice to meet you, Craig. I'm Lori. I'd shake your hand, but..."

He smiled and a devilish glint lit his eyes. "I sure wouldn't complain if you did." He leaned forward. "Would you like some tanning lotion on the front?"

"Umm..." She'd barely met the man, but the thought of his hands stroking her body made her melt. Hot liquid pooled inside her.

He pushed himself from the chair and grabbed the tube of lotion. Seconds later, his strong, warm hands smeared lotion on her legs and started working it in, first on her calves, then up her thighs. As he neared her crotch, his hands curved around and slipped to her hips, then his palms worked their way up her stomach, then over her ribs. Next, he stroked her shoulders and curved over the edge of her bikini top, careful not to shift it.

He smiled wickedly, but he finished with a dab on her nose, then he returned to his chair. A perfect gentleman. *Too perfect*, a part of her grumbled. Why couldn't he have tugged away her top and massaged her breasts with his warm, capable hands? The thought made her nipples pucker painfully.

He tipped his hat over his eyes and relaxed.

Damn. She wanted him to seduce her, but if any seducing was going to happen, it would have to be her doing it. Unfortunately, she just wasn't that bold. She imagined walking over to him, straddling his hips and settling her pussy down on his long, hard erection. She'd start to move up and down, stroking him with her crotch. She'd drop her bikini top and he'd lean forward and take her nipple in his mouth.

Oh, God, she wanted to fuck him, but the man would think her an absolute sex maniac if she just jumped his bones.

She leaned back and closed her eyes, settling for daydreaming about him. She imagined his hands touching her, stroking down to her bathing suite bottoms, slipping his finger under the elastic. The sun beat down on her skin, warming her, making her sleepy. Her mind wandered.

The long, hard cock thrust into her. She sucked in a deep breath. *Oh, Drake, that feels so good.* It thrust again. Harder. Oh, dear God, Drake, shove it in deeper.

The climax began, then twitched and slipped away. She groaned, then shifted, reaching out for him. Something jarred her arm. Her eyelids flicked open and she realized she was on the lounge chair by Marie's pool. Her elbow had banged against the armrest. A rustling of cloth grabbed her attention and she gazed to the left. Craig—Drake?—lay on a chair opposite her, watching her, his hand on his long, naked cock, stroking it.

Embarrassment flushed through her. She pretended to keep her eyes closed and she turned her head the other way.

"Marie?" she murmured, intending to alert him to the fact she was awake without embarrassing them both.

"Marie isn't here."

"Drake?" Slowly, she lifted her head. When she turned toward him, a towel rested over his lap, covering his incredible hard-on.

"Lori, you were calling out in your sleep."

"Was I?" Her stomach twisted. What had he heard?

She pushed herself to a sitting position and his blue-gray eyes darkened to smoldering charcoal. *Oh, God.* She glanced down to see her naked breasts on display, nipples at full attention. She'd forgotten about her loose top.

She scrambled to grab it.

"Please don't." He licked his lips, his gaze caressing her breasts.

She stared at him, mesmerized by the look of compelling desire in his eyes.

"You're so beautiful like that."

He stood up and approached her. His towel fell to the ground and the head of his cock had pushed free of his suit.

She sat frozen as he reached for her; pulling her to her feet and into his arms. Her breasts pressed against his hard-muscled chest, the sprinkling of dark curls prickling against her nipples. He claimed her mouth with a wild hunger, stirring her own desperate craving. She pushed her tongue between his lips, tasting mint. He groaned, then twirled his tongue against hers, the two twining like frenzied tango dancers.

Was this Craig, Drake's identical twin brother, or had that just been a dream? His hands stroked over her bare back, then cupped her bottom. It had to be. She couldn't stand the torture of having to push him away. This had to be Craig.

But what if it was Drake? She should ask him, make sure—

He pulled her pelvis tight against his straining erection and her vagina ached painfully with need. Sane thought slipped away. His hands slipped around her waist and he lifted her. She wrapped her legs around him as he carried her, her eyes closed as their mouths moved together. They shifted downward and she felt hot water on her legs. The steps of the hot tub.

He settled her on the edge of the tub, the tumbled stone warm against her buttocks.

"God, you're a beautiful woman." He stripped off her bathing suit bottom and eased her legs open, then gazed at her dripping wet pussy. One hand caressed her thigh as the other slid over her breast, fondling it. He lapped at the other nipple with his tongue and she gasped at the erotic feeling. A feeling she'd been craving forever.

He took her nipple in his mouth and sucked, softly at first, then deeper. She arched forward. His hands slid down her sides to her hips, then he released her nipple and smiled at her. He kissed the base of her neck, then down the center of her chest to her navel, which he licked and kissed thoroughly. She arched her pelvis, anxious for pleasures yet to come.

His journey continued. He kissed to her curls, then moved sideways and down her inner thigh. She opened her legs wider and stroked her fingers through his hair. He teased her mercilessly, coming closer to her aching pussy each time, then careening away, until she could barely stand it.

"Oh, God, don't make me beg."

He smiled broadly. "I wouldn't do that."

The tip of his tongue dabbed lightly at her folds of flesh, barely touching her, then flicked away.

She ached with need. "Please."

"Okay, maybe I like you begging a little."

"Please, Drake, please kiss my pussy. Please make me come."

His smile faded a little, but still he eased forward and licked the length of her slit. A wondrous elation filled her. He licked again and she almost cried out at the pure bliss of his intimate touch. His tongue nudged her clit and she did cry out, but a nagging voice inside her screamed over the thudding of her pulse. *You can't do this with your best friend's husband.*

CHAPTER 3

Lori gulped, and grasped his head, easing him back.

"What is it, Lori?"

"Tell me first, are you Craig, Drake's twin brother?"

His dark eyes grew serious and he took her lips in a maelstrom of passion.

"Who do you want me to be, Lori?" His hand slid between her legs and his fingers slipped into her moist opening. "I'll be anyone you want." His deep, throaty words wafted over her and the haze of passion claimed her.

He replaced his fingers with his tongue and cajoled her clit until sparks flared through her, igniting her insides with a wildfire of pleasure.

She clung to his head, holding him so tightly against her she wondered that he didn't drown in her juices.

"Oh, God, I'm coming."

His tongue rippled and pulsed against her, sending her over the edge of pleasure and into the realm of fantasy bliss.

As the world quivered around her, she clung to him, his dark, wavy hair curled around her fingers. She became aware of his hands around her waist, holding her steady.

He dragged her against his body and hugged her close, then met her lips in an explosive kiss.

"Lori, I'm going to make love to you now." He took her hand and rested it on his bare cock head.

"Not until I do this." She wrapped her fingers around his cock, shoving his bathing suit downward, out of the way, then licked the tip.

He grinned widely.

"Heaven forbid I deny you."

He stripped off the garment, then sat on the edge of the tub. Her lips wrapped around him and she swirled her tongue around the ridge of the corona.

He felt so wonderful under her tongue, the smooth texture of him a delight. She toyed with him for several minutes, then sucked him into her mouth, eliciting a sharp gasp. She sucked hard, then bobbed her head up and down, taking him deep, then sliding almost off him, then deep again. She released him then slid her hands the length of his thighs as she eased his legs wide apart, so she could lick his balls, then up the length of his shaft.

A drop of fluid oozed from the tiny hole in the tip of his cock head. She captured it with the tip of her tongue, then snared his neck and brought his face to hers. She slid her finger into his mouth and opened his lips, then pushed her tongue inside, sharing his taste with him. He licked her tongue. Satisfied, she returned to his glorious, rigid cock. She sucked him deep while fondling his balls. She stroked his perineum, right behind his balls, and felt him stiffen. His cock seemed to swell.

She wrapped her hands around him and slid her mouth off him.

"Baby, let it loose. I'll handle it." She swallowed him to the hilt, squeezing him tight.

She stroked behind his balls and sucked and squeezed his

cock until she felt him tense and grunt. Hot liquid spurted against the back of her throat. She gazed up at him. Seeing his face contorted in pleasure turned her on immensely. After several seconds, the stream of semen slowed then stopped. She licked around the tip of his cock, then slowly released him.

He grabbed her and dragged her to him, capturing her mouth with a fervent need. Did he want to taste his own seed?

No, he wanted to taste her. She could tell by the tender passion in his touch. When he released her, the loving look in his eyes confirmed it.

If this was actually Drake… If he was falling for her…

No, she wouldn't go there. She wouldn't allow herself to believe she could break up her friend's marriage.

She couldn't entertain the possibility that this was Drake. Not while she was still so needy.

She stroked her breasts, then plucked at the nipples. He sucked one into his mouth while he watched her stimulate the other. She felt his cock inflate, hardening as it rested against her ribs. He lifted her out of the water and set her on the edge of the tub again.

He eased into the water and positioned himself in front of her. His gaze locked onto hers.

"I'm going to make love to you now, Lori."

"Yes." She stared at his intense blue eyes, mesmerized.

"I'm going to give you the most explosive orgasm you've ever experienced."

"Bring it on."

He eased her legs apart and stroked her slick pussy. The head of his erection bumped against her, then the tip of his cock head eased into her opening. He pulled away and she whimpered, then he eased forward again. This time the head slipped fully inside. He eased out again. She wrapped her legs around his waist and tried to draw him in deeper as she shifted forward. His cock head pushed inside her and he slipped in part of the shaft, then eased out again.

"Don't rush me, sweetheart," he murmured against her ear, then kissed the base of her neck.

She released a shaky breath at the pleasure quivering through her. He shifted forward and back several more times before he filled her completely, then he held her tight against him, every iron-hard inch of him inside her. She squeezed him and he drew out, his cock head dragging on her sensitive inner flesh, stimulating her with intense pleasure.

"Are you ready, baby?" he asked, as he almost pulled out, then paused.

"Yes. Now," she pleaded.

He thrust forward, deep and hard. She gasped at the exquisite sensation. He pulled back and thrust again.

"I'm so close." She clung to him as he pulled back and thrust again.

He pumped slowly at first, then picked up speed. Her breathing accelerated with each stroke of his erection along her inner passage.

"Do you want it harder?"

"Yes." The word came out on a heavy breath.

"Do you want it deeper?"

"Oh, God, yes."

He drove into her. Her eyelids dropped closed and spirals of stars swirled through her consciousness. Pleasure pulsed through her, building to an incredible pounding cataclysm.

"I... I'm coming." She groaned, then sucked in a deep breath.

He thrust and held her close as hot semen exploded into her, flooding her insides, propelling her to ecstasy. He twisted his pelvis in a spiral and another wave of pleasure catapulted through her, then held her on a long standing wave as he swirled his rigid cock inside her, around and around until she could hardly breath with the sheer joy of orgasm. The best orgasm of her life.

She fell against him, a boneless mass.

"My God, that was the best... I mean, I've never..." She just couldn't say it. It felt too cliché.

"I'm flattered, but I couldn't have done it without you."

He tipped her chin up and kissed her. She glanced at him and the warmth in his eyes stirred her heart. She wanted him again. Right now.

But guilt nudged through her. She had to find out. She had to ask him—

"Ahem..."

Her head jerked to the side to see Drake staring down at them.

CHAPTER 4

Lori froze.

If that was Drake, this *must* be Craig holding her in his arms. Relief washed through her, chased away by embarrassment as she realized she sat on the edge of his hot tub, naked, with his twin brother's cock buried deep inside her.

"Brother, you have certainly found yourself a prize."

"Lori, if you liked one brother so much..." Craig's finger slid to her clit and he nudged it gently, "I think you might like two even better."

"But I..."

Drake's hands cupped her breasts.

"... shouldn't..." Reason and logic slipped away as her eyelids fell closed. Drake's warm hands sent shimmering heat through her.

Drake stepped into the tub and Craig's cock slipped out of her as he shifted a little to one side. She felt the delightful sensation of each nipple being drawn into a warm mouth. One man sucked while the other dabbed and licked. One swirled while the other nipped lightly with his teeth.

Craig shifted to the side as Drake's lips claimed hers.

Vaguely, she watched Craig climb the steps of the tub and run toward the house, his cock bobbing up and down, but Drake's mouth ravishing hers, and his hands exploring her breasts, kept her busy. A moment later, Craig's welcome hands stroked her back as he sat beside her. He opened a tube and squeezed liquid onto his hands, then began stroking his cock. He took her hand and stroked it over him. Slick and warm. It must be the lubricant Marie had told her about; the one that warmed when it came into contact with skin.

His hands slid between her legs as Drake continued to fondle her breasts.

"Baby, I want to fuck your ass," Craig murmured into her ear, his breath sending tingles along her neck and down her spine. "Will you let me do that?"

"I…" She licked her lips. She'd wanted to try anal sex, but the thought made her nervous.

He nuzzled her temple

"I'll be very gentle. I promise."

She nodded. She knew he would.

She stood up, the hot, bubbling water swirling around her legs, and she turned around, then grasped the edge of the tub and leaned forward.

"Let me help," Drake said.

He covered his fingers with the lubricant and slid one finger inside her, then another. They slid right in, warm and slippery. He moved them in and out, stretching her slightly, then he slid in a third finger.

She felt Craig's cock bob against her thigh. Drake withdrew his fingers and Craig positioned his erection against her opening. Hot and slick, it slid in, forcing her open. Slowly, he eased inside, stretching her, until his cock head filled her. He stopped and drew her back against him, then stroked her breasts.

She leaned forward.

"Give me more."

He pushed, slowly, until his whole cock was inside her. It was a little uncomfortable at first, but as Craig stroked her ass and Drake caressed her breasts, she relaxed.

She grasped Drake's arm and drew him forward as she patted the side of the tub.

"Sit here," she instructed.

He pushed himself up on the edge and she directed him sideways until he was right in front of her. She leaned forward and swallowed his dick right to the base, her tongue swirling around his shaft.

"Oh, honey." Drake groaned.

Craig slid back, then eased forward again. The feel of his cock head dragging on her anal passage felt fantastic. She sucked on Drake, hard, then squeezed him, her hands lightly caressing his balls.

Craig pushed in again, then eased away. Both cocks, impossibly hard within her, made her feel wild and passionate. Her head bobbed up and down, faster and faster, until finally, Drake stilled her movements.

"Honey, slow down. I don't want to come yet."

He stroked her cheek and leaned forward to kiss her temple.

"In fact, I've got a great idea."

She glanced up at him, then released his cock from her mouth.

"What is it?"

Craig still slid in and out of her ass with gentle strokes.

"Craig, stay inside her and sit on the edge."

Craig's hands tightened around her waist as he pushed fully into her, then he eased her backwards with him. As he leaned against the tub wall, Drake helped lift her as Craig shifted onto the edge. Now she sat on Craig's cock while he held her legs wide.

Drake stroked her clit and she moaned, then positioned himself in front of her, holding his huge erection in his hand. He pressed it against her slick opening and eased inside.

"Oh, yes," she gasped.

He pushed in, deeper and deeper. Her breathing accelerated as she felt both openings stretched by these two enormous cocks. She'd never felt anything so incredible.

He started moving inside her with long, slow thrusts, at the same time lifting her up and down on Craig's cock, which was still buried deep inside her ass. The two penises seemed to stroke each other inside her. Drake flicked her clit with his finger again and she cried out, then catapulted into orgasm.

"Oh, my God, I coming."

"That's right, baby," Craig murmured against her ear, his voice heavy. "Come for us."

Her head rolled back and she moaned, intense pleasure spearing through her.

Craig's hand covered her breast and squeezed as his ragged breathing filled her ear. Drake thrust faster, stiffened, and spurted into her vagina, then Craig grunted and spewed inside her ass.

Their movements slowed to a stop and the three of them clung to each other, gasping for breath.

"Oh, my God, Lori."

Marie's voice startled Lori. Her face flamed and she realized she had just been caught fucking her best friend's husband.

CHAPTER 5

Lori swiveled her head to face her friend.

"Marie, I—"

She stopped mid-sentence when she saw Marie standing arm-in-arm with Drake.

Another Drake.

Relief washed through her at the thought she hadn't cheated with her best friend's husband, followed immediately by intense embarrassment at having been caught naked, with two cocks inside her.

"Who are you?" Lori asked the 'Drake' in front of her.

"I'm Abel."

He swirled inside her and she had to agree, he was definitely *able*.

Craig eased forward to slip into the water, and Abel drew her to his body to hide her nakedness from view. The two cocks slipped free under the water.

"Don't be embarrassed, Lori," Marie said. Her fingers slid over her bikini top and toyed with her nipples as she spoke. "I found it incredibly hot watching you making out with two guys." She glanced at Drake. "Right, honey?"

"God, yes. I'm glad you like my brothers, Lori."

"In fact, I'd love to see you with three," said Marie.

Lori's face burned, surprised at her friend's reaction.

"Sorry, Marie, I don't have a third handy."

Marie glanced at Drake with a sly grin. "I do."

Lori's eyes widened and Drake's smile grew broad.

"What do you think, love?" Marie asked Drake.

The smoldering look in his dark, blue eyes gave no doubt as to his feelings.

"I am at Lori's service."

"I, uh…" Here was her dream, to make love with Drake, and with Marie's permission. She nodded.

"Guys, what do you say," Drake asked his brothers.

"I'm definitely up for it," Abel answered.

Lori could see his cock rising under the water.

"Me, too." Craig stroked her stomach as he pressed against her back, his hardening cock pressing along the length of her buttocks.

Lori lit up inside with excitement as Craig scooped her into his arms and carried her from the hot tub, Abel following close behind. Craig laid her on one of the lounge chairs, then knelt on the ground beside the chair. Abel knelt on the other side of the chair.

Lori watched as Drake approached her, his blue eyes caressing the length of her naked, slick body. He knelt in front of her and leaned forward, kissing her navel, his tongue dabbing inside.

She sighed at his touch. Abel leaned over and lapped at one of her nipples. It thrust against his tongue. Craig leaned forward and drew her other nipple into his hot mouth.

"Oh, yes, that feels wonderful." Lori sighed, loving the feel of three busy tongues pleasuring her.

Drake kissed across her belly to her hip, his hands stroked her inner thighs. She undulated under his caresses, her knees parting. His fingers parted her lower lips and he dipped his head to her slit and licked.

"Oh… yes."

Craig's hand slid around her breast and he lifted it, squeezing lightly as he kissed her nipple.

Drake licked her clit and Lori exhaled sharply. Abel's hand stroked her breast, his thumb teasing the nub as he nuzzled her neck.

Drake vibrated his tongue against her tight button and she gasped at the intense pleasure bursting through her. His fingers traced her thighs, then cupped her bottom and held her snug against his mouth as his tongue bored into her.

Marie's hands stroked across Lori's temples, combing through her long, auburn hair as she watched Drake intently.

Drake jabbed his tongue into Lori's vagina and swirled around the inside, then licked her clit again. His fingers slipped inside her, stroking along the wall of her vagina. Intense need built within her. The g-spot. He'd found it and worked it with expert skill.

A moan escaped her before she even realized it. The exquisite feel of his tongue on her clit, the mounting pleasure from his gentle strokes insider her, the feel of hot male on each of her breasts, even the feel of Marie stroking her hair, all combined to send her screaming over the edge, sparks flaring inside her and exploding in a short but intense orgasm. Liquid flooded between her legs. Drake leaned back and smiled smugly.

She rewarded him with a long languid smile of her own. Drake drew her to her feet. Craig and Abel pushed two chairs together and sat down. Drake guided Lori to get on all fours in front of them and he guided his cock to her wet slit and eased inside. Her eyelids fell closed.

"Mmm." She had dreamed of Drake's cock inside her for so long, and now she was experiencing it for the first time.

He buried himself deep inside her and held still. She opened her eyes to see two lovely, erect cocks in front of her. She licked one then the other. Marie groaned as Lori positioned her mouth over Abel's cock and slowly swallowed him whole. Marie sat on a chair behind them, one hand under her bikini top and her other slipping inside her bottoms.

Lori slid up Abel's shaft, then swirled her tongue around the ridge of his cock head. He moaned and stroked her hair. She released him, wrapping her hand around his shaft and pumping up and down while she nibbled Craig into her mouth, then sucked him hard.

Drake started to move inside her. Lori started a rhythm with her hand sliding up and down on Abel and her mouth on Craig. Drake followed her rhythm as he pumped inside her. Marie had stripped off her bathing suit, her large, round breasts heaving with her accelerated breathing, and her fingers toying with one dusky nipple while three fingers of her other hand pumped inside her to the same rhythm.

As Drake's enormous cock slid in and out of Lori, she felt an intense sexual synergy building between the five of them.

"Do you like that, Lori?" Drake asked as he thrust into her.

She nodded, bobbing up and down on Craig's cock. She shifted to Abel's, pumping Craig's with her hand.

"She likes it deep and hard," Craig said, stroking the hair behind her ear.

Drake thrust again, driving deep inside her.

Marie crept up beside Craig.

"Let me help," Marie said. She leaned back across one of Craig's knees and lapped at Lori's nipple, then sucked it.

"Ohhh…" Lori loved the gentle feel of Marie's lips on her breast.

Craig stroked Marie's breast, then slid his fingers into her slit. Marie gasped, releasing Lori's nipple, but quickly drew it back into her mouth again.

As Lori sucked on Abel's cock, she watched Craig's hands stroke Marie's clit. Lori released Abel's cock and Marie slipped off Lori's breast. Lori kissed Marie, brushing her lips with her tongue, then shifted to Craig's cock, her body sliding over Marie's, her breasts cushioned on the soft, smooth skin of Marie's stomach. Drake continued to thrust into Lori's hot pussy and she squeezed him. Marie dropped her head back and grasped Abel's cock in her hands. He shifted so he could slide his cock into her mouth. Marie slid her hands around his hips then, under Marie's direction, he shifted his pelvis forward and back, fucking her mouth.

Drake thrust hard and groaned. Lori could feel him swell inside her. The sexual energy sizzled through her and she felt the tide of pleasure rising. Abel groaned.

"Baby, you're so good," Craig murmured, stroking her hair.

The hard cock inside her pulled on her vagina, then thrust deep. A tidal wave of erotic sensation plummeted her over the edge as Drake groaned, then released a wash of hot semen inside her. She moaned, then cried out as Abel reached under her and tweaked her clit. Marie moaned her release and Abel grunted and jerked into her mouth.

"Oh, God, yes, Lori." Craig grunted as his hot fluid spurted into her throat.

Lori slumped against Marie. Drake stroked Lori's buttocks, and then slipped out of her. As soon as Lori released Craig's cock from her mouth, he drew her into his arms and kissed her. She snuggled against him. Mmm, she could get used to this.

Abel helped Marie up and Drake slid his arm around her waist, a big smile on his face.

"Well, that was exciting, but it wasn't exactly all three of you making love to Lori," Marie commented.

"You distracted us a little, my love," Drake murmured against her hair.

Craig took Lori's hand and led her to the low stone retaining wall behind the patio.

"We certainly want to keep our hostess happy," he whispered.

CHAPTER 6

Lori's heart hammered as Craig positioned her in a sitting position on the wall, then shifted between her legs and dipped his semi-erect cock into her.

Abel stepped up beside him. Craig thrust three times, his cock swelling inside her, then withdrew. Abel took his place, pushing his almost rigid cock into her. Drake joined them. Abel thrust three times then withdrew, his cock now completely rigid. Drake thrust into her next, three times, just like his brothers. Craig started the pattern again.

Lori felt the heat rise in her. Abel slipped into her. She didn't know how long she'd last with this kind of attention. Drake slipped in next. She closed her eyes and felt the cocks thrust and withdraw, thrust and withdraw. The changing of cocks gave her a little cooling off space, but not much.

A new cock slipped into her. She opened her eyes. Craig. She wasn't sure how she could tell, but she could.

"Oh, this is so sexy!" Marie sat beside her, her legs spread as she fingered herself watching each new cock dip into Lori.

Abel thrust into Lori next.

"Oh, God, I'm going to…"

He tightened his arms around her and thrust deeper. She gasped and exploded in a gargantuan climax as he groaned against her.

He kissed her and withdrew. His limp penis happily flopped against his balls.

Craig pushed into her and thrust, drawing her close. She exploded in orgasm again. Craig eased out of her, still stiff as a steel rod.

Drake sat down on the wall and Craig lifted her onto Drake's lap. Drake's cock pushed against her anus, then eased inside.

"Oh, yes." She stretched around him, welcoming the feel of his big, hard cock inside her.

Craig stepped in front of her and pushed his erection into her at an excruciatingly slow pace, teasing her. Once he was buried to the hilt, he cupped her cheeks and stared deep into her eyes. Drake grasped her hips and lifted her up and down as Craig thrust in and out, then picked up the pace until he was pounding into her. The pleasure intensified as the two penises thrust into her at the same time.

"Oh, God." Her voice sounded close to tears, so intense were the sensations.

Abel stood watching them until she grasped his penis and drew him close, then swallowed his prick into her mouth. She sucked mercilessly as the other two continued to thrust inside her. At the mounting pleasure, she moaned and he slipped from her mouth. She grasped him in her hands and pumped.

"Oh, God, I'm coming…" She moaned, loud and long as explosions of ecstasy shuddered through her.

Hot semen flooded her in both passages as the two men groaned and thrust. They collapsed together, her hand slowing on Abel's still rock-hard erection.

Lori felt a soft hand slide the cock from her grasp.

"I'll take care of this, honey," Marie said.

Craig lifted Lori into his arms, the penis behind her slipping free. He sat down on the wall, cuddling Lori against his chest, his cock still inside her. She wrapped her legs around his waist and squeezed him inside. He twitched, still semi-erect.

As she rested in the warmth of his arms, she watched as Abel sat beside Marie and stroked her breasts. Marie stood up and took his hands, then turned her back to him, resting his hands on her breasts. He cupped them and fondled while kissing her neck.

"Abel, push that incredible cock into my ass."

Abel smiled and wrapped his hand around his cock and positioned it.

Drake stepped in front of her and kissed her as Abel pushed into her.

"Oh, yeah." She licked her lips and stared into Drake's eyes. Even though another man had just penetrated her, there was no mistaking the love between Drake and Marie. They might share, but they wouldn't stray.

Abel wrapped his hands around her hips and eased her backwards, then sat on the wall. She opened her legs and Drake stepped forward to slide inside her. Lori marveled at the erotic sight of Drake's long, hard cock slipping into Marie's wet opening.

"Oh, Honey, this feels so incredible," Marie cooed.

The depth of passion Lori saw in Marie's eyes melted her heart. Drake held Marie's gaze as he pulled back, then eased forward again, the whole time watching her, seeing her pleasure grow as the two penises thrust into her at the same time.

Watching the three of them undulating up and down, Marie's face contorting in pleasure, turned Lori on immensely. Craig, too, from the feel of his cock swelling inside her. She started to move on him, his hardening cock and the sound of passion beside her propelling her to a quick and intense orgasm. She slumped against him, but he wrapped his hands around her waist and lifted her. Up and down, up and down, and she felt another wave pummel her with pleasure. Just as that eased up, another hit.

"Oh, God, I'm coming again."

Marie moaned and the two men inside her groaned. Craig grunted and squirted inside Lori, the sensation of his hot fluid washing through her sending her over the edge again. She clung to him, totally exhausted. They all gasped for air, fully sated.

CHAPTER 7

A half hour later, they all sat in the pool, sipping cold pina coladas.

Lori sat on the entry steps in the shallow water, Craig beside her, holding her tight to his side. She felt unsettled, still guilty that she'd lusted over her best friend's husband.

"I'm glad you two finally got together," Marie said, smiling at them.

"What do you mean, finally?"

"Well, when Craig first saw your picture, he told me he'd seen you a few times at the subway station and he'd wanted to meet you, but it never worked out."

Lori turned to face him and smiled. "I'd seen you, too. In fact, I started dreaming about you, but I thought you were Drake."

Marie choked on her drink.

Oh, God, Lori realized she'd just admitted her lust for Marie's husband.

"You thought it was Drake." Marie stared at her with wide eyes then, to Lori's complete amazement, her friend started to laugh. "No wonder you've been avoiding us."

"Marie, I'm so sorry. I didn't mean to—"

Marie waved away Lori's words.

"Oh, sweetie, of course you didn't. That's why you avoided us." She smiled in reassurance. "Lori, you can't help how you feel. You didn't act on it."

Now it was Lori's turn to choke.

"Okay, so maybe you did, but that was at my insistence."

Lori shook her head. "When Abel joined Craig and me… I thought…"

Marie laughed. "I'm not going to get mad about that. The situation was pretty bizarre. Anyway, sweetie, I know you would never do anything to hurt me, and that includes never coming between Drake and I. That's why I didn't mind letting Drake make love to you. It was all in the sense of adventure."

Abel held up his glass. "And what an adventure it was."

"You said it," Drake responded.

"Anyway," Marie continued, "Anyone can see that you're head over heels for Craig, and vice versa."

Craig kissed her shoulder.

"For my part, it's true," he murmured in her ear.

She glanced up at him, seeing the tender look of love in his eyes. She sighed, knowing this was a man she could spend a lifetime with. A man she had certainly dreamed about.

Craig. It had been Craig all along.

"Yes. Me too." She brought her lips to his, sliding her tongue into his mouth.

His arms tightened around her and he kissed her passionately. She tugged his hand to her breast and sighed as he cupped her. He stripped off her top and kissed her cold, wet nipples.

Marie watched as her friend leaned back, her breasts floating in the water as Craig stripped off her bikini bottoms.

He lifted her lower body and licked her clit. Lori moaned in response.

Drake's arms tightened around Marie and his growing cock pressed into her back. Abel watched Craig and Lori, his hand drawing his huge cock free from the confining fabric of his bathing suit.

"I think we should let those two enjoy each other. I guess I'll have to entertain you boys myself," Marie said as she freed the clasp of her top, exposing her aching breasts.

Drake stroked one and Abel stroked the other. Moments later, Abel held her against his chest, stroking her nipples to rigid pebbles as Drake slipped his hard cock inside her and thrust deep.

Pleasure cascaded through her, as Abel eased his prick into her ass. She wondered if Lori would help her find a match for Abel.

Passion washed the thought away as an orgasm surged through her.

THREE MEN AND A BRIDE

Now that you've read Lori and Craig's story, maybe you'd like to go back and learn more about Marie and Drake in this prequel to Three.

What do you do when you can't stop lusting after your new husband's two gorgeous brothers?

"You look nervous?" Marie's new husband, Drake, glanced at her as he sped along the highway toward their new home.

"A little," she responded.

Her stomach fluttered. Of course she was nervous.

She and Drake had had a whirlwind romance while on a singles' tour in Costa Rica and, throwing caution to the wind, had gotten married. It was the craziest thing she'd ever done. Not that she had any doubt that she loved Drake. Truly and deeply. Sometimes you just knew when it was right.

And this was right.

Drake reached for her hand. "Everything will be fine."

But now came the reality of life.

They had just gotten off the plane an hour ago and now they were going home. But to his house which she'd never seen. They had discussed it and it made sense that she move into his two-storey, four bedroom house rather than her tiny one bedroom apartment. He had offered to go back to her place first so she could pick up some things, maybe even stay overnight tonight so she'd feel more settled, but they were both tired after a day of travel so she just wanted to settle in. And she'd been excited to see her new home.

Now she wondered if she should have taken him up on his offer. Spending a night in her own place would have allowed her to get acclimatized to being back in Toronto again.

Too late now. And she was sure she would love his place and feel right at home. As long as she was by Drake's side she would be happy.

"Craig and Abel will probably call this evening to come over and meet you. If you're not up to it, I'll defer."

She nodded. "Tomorrow would be better."

Drake had told her about his brothers and she was intrigued. She had never met triplets before. She couldn't imagine talking to three men who looked exactly alike, espe-

41

cially when they all looked like her husband. It would be a strange experience.

Drake took an off ramp and about ten minutes later, turned onto a quiet, tree-lined street. She peered out the window at the lovely homes along the road. Most of the yards had mature trees, professional landscaping, and brilliant displays of flowers. He turned into a wide driveway with its two-car garage and she gazed at the large brick house with the stone path leading through an array of blossoming plants to a welcoming front door.

"It's beautiful."

He smiled as he leaned in to give her a kiss.

"You stay right there while I get the car door." He got out of the car and opened her door, then took her hand. As soon as she was standing, he scooped her into his arms.

She laughed. "Hey, I can walk you know."

But he carried her along the stone path. "And deprive me of carrying my bride over the threshold?"

She gazed at his rugged face, his square jaw lightly shadowed, his blue eyes twinkling, and she stroked his raspy cheek.

"You're such a romantic."

A chuckle rumbled from deep in his chest. "And that's why you love me, right?"

She leaned in and nuzzled his neck, remembering how for their first date, he'd set up a romantic candlelit dinner on a secluded beach, and once they'd started seeing each other, he'd brought her a beautiful blossom for her hair every night. And the first time they'd made love, he'd arranged a romantic setting by filling the room with candles and vases of lovely, fragrant flowers, had soft music playing, and chilled champagne at the ready.

Not that she'd needed any of that. After three days of his attentive courting, she'd been so hot for him she could barely stop herself from ripping off his clothes as soon as they'd stepped into the room that night.

And her anticipation had been worth it.

"Well, my sweet man, there are a great number of reasons why I love you." She nipped his skin between her teeth, feeling that same desire rushing through her. "And I'm hoping you'll treat me to my favorite one as soon as we get inside."

He growled and captured her lips, showing he knew exactly what she had in mind.

They reached the front door and he fumbled in his pocket for the key, then opened the door and stepped inside.

"Hey, great, thanks."

She felt herself scooped from Drake's arms and suddenly glanced from him to another male face. Her hands automatically hooked around his neck to steady herself. Her heart jumped a beat. It was Drake's face. Or rather, one of his brother's.

"Great gift, bro. I hope you have another for Craig."

She glanced at Drake again and then back at... this must be Abel.

"No such luck, man," Drake said. "This one's all mine. Marie, this is my brother Abel." He glanced at his brother. "Where's Craig?"

"In the kitchen," Abel answered. "We thought you'd be hungry so he whipped up some chili."

"I need to get the luggage." Drake kissed Marie on the cheek and smiled. "You're in good hands here. I'll be right back, okay?"

No. It wasn't okay. It was very unnerving to be in this strange man's arms, even though he looked exactly like her husband. In fact, *especially* because he looked exactly like Drake. But she nodded, ignoring the nervous flutter in her stomach.

"Abel, get Marie a drink, will you? Then show her around the main floor."

"Sure thing, bro."

"And maybe put me down," she suggested.

Abel grinned at her. "Tired of me already, eh."

He lowered her to her feet and she released his neck, then smoothed down the skirt of her sundress.

Drake had disappeared out the front door and now she stood alone with his brother.

"I could use that drink," she said.

"Sure thing. That way." He pointed to a doorway and gestured for her to precede him.

She walked through it to a large gourmet kitchen with dark wood cabinets, glossy granite counters and slate floors. The wonderful, spicy aroma of the chili filled the room.

"Hey, there. You must be Marie." Another Drake stepped from behind the counter and held out his hand.

She placed her hand in his, thrown totally off balance by the feel of his big, warm hand enveloping hers as he shook it.

"You must be Craig." The words came out as a croak and she cleared her throat.

Instead of releasing her hand, he pulled her against him, his arms tightening around her in a warm embrace.

"Welcome to the family." He squeezed, then released her.

She gazed up at his smiling face and, for a moment, could almost believe this was actually Drake standing in front of her. She smiled faintly at him. Oh, God, they looked so much alike. And they were probably alike in a lot of ways. Their voices were the same. Their physiques were the same, all three quite fit and muscular. Her brain then darted to where she forbade it to go. They were identical triplets, so all parts of their anatomies would be the same.

Visions of Drake's exceptionally large, erect cock shimmered through her brain and suddenly she could imagine

Craig standing before her, with his big cock standing erect. She could imagine wrapping her hand around it, then Abel stepping beside Craig, his cock swelling to attention, too. She would wrap her hand around his, too, then crouch down and—

La la la la la.... She could not think about this. She forced her brain to change direction and glanced around her new kitchen.

"Drink?" she squeaked.

"I think we're overwhelming her," Abel said behind her. "We've got beer, wine, and a pitcher of marguerites."

"Marguerite, please."

Craig went to the stove to check the pot of chili and Abel handed her glass tinkling with ice. She sipped the tart drink and sighed.

"So how about that tour?" Abel said.

"Oh," her hand tightened around the cold glass. "Maybe later. Right now I'd just like to sit down."

Abel led her to a bright, spacious living room with dark brown wood furniture and rust colored couch and chairs. Craig followed them a beer in his hand. She sat on the couch and the brothers sat in the two armchairs facing her.

"So it must have been great getting married in Costa Rica," Craig said.

She nodded. "It was. The setting was idyllic." She sipped her drink, not feeling particularly chatty.

"We're sorry we couldn't fly down," Abel said.

"Oh, no, we understand." She sipped her drink again, feeling like she was seeing double with the two identical Drake's sitting in front of her.

"Did any of your family come?" Abel asked.

"No. My parents are divorced so I didn't really ask them. It would have been awkward. I would have liked my best friend, Lori to come, but she wasn't able to." She turned on her phone and pulled up her favorite picture of her and Lori. "That's her." She handed the phone to Abel.

"Very pretty." He handed the phone to Craig.

Craig glanced at the picture, then his focus intensified.

A sound in the entryway signaled that Drake had come in with the luggage.

"Hey, layabouts." Drake popped his head in the doorway. "Some help here?"

Marie stood up, but Drake chuckled. "Not you, sweetheart. I mean my lazy brothers."

"Who's lazy? Didn't we come and make dinner for you and you new bride?" Craig said, a big smile on his face.

"And cut the grass while you were gone. Plus watering all those flowers of yours," Abel added.

"And I am most appreciative. Now maybe you wouldn't mind carrying a few bags upstairs, so my new bride can settle in a little sooner."

Craig slapped Drake's shoulder as he passed. "Admit it, man. You just want to get back to your beautiful new wife."

He grinned. "Well, can you blame me?"

"Sit, bro," Abel said as he headed down the hallway. "We've got this covered."

Drake disappeared for a moment, then returned with a beer in his hand. He sat down beside her and she slid her hand into his.

"Miss me?" he asked.

She nodded.

"Hey, what's wrong?" His relaxed expression turned to one of concern.

"Oh, nothing. I'm just really tired. I'm really happy to meet your brothers, but…" What could she say? Send them away?

"Do you want me to ask the guys to leave?"

"I… uh… well, Craig made dinner and all."

46

"Okay, quick dinner, then I'll tell them I'm beat. They'll understand."

She smiled, tightening her hand around his. "I would like to get out of this dress."

His lips turned up in a lascivious grin. "And I would like to help you do just that."

He pulled her close and captured her lips. Her tongue met his and slid into his warm mouth. Her body responded to him as it always did. Melting heat and raging desire.

"Well, clearly the honeymoon is *not* over." From the khaki pants he wore, she knew it was Abel.

"Maybe we should leave these two lovebirds alone," Craig said.

"Nonsense. You made dinner for us. Let's enjoy it together." Drake stood up. "In fact, I'm starving. Why don't we eat now?"

He held out his hand to Marie and led her toward the kitchen.

"I'll serve it up," Abel offered.

Craig grabbed cutlery from the drawer set it on the table in the eating area while Abel scooped the steaming chili into bowls.

"Smells great, Craig. As usual."

She sat down at the table and Drake settled beside her.

While they ate, the brothers talked about sports and made some tentative plans to visit their family cottage together. She ate in silence, totally overwhelmed by the sight of three copies of her husband chatting animatedly together.

Drake cleared the empty bowls from the table and the three men had the kitchen cleaned up before she had a chance to offer help.

Drake's arm slid around her. "We really appreciate the reception, guys, but we're both tired after the trip."

"We can take a hint." Craig grabbed Drake in a big hug and patted his back. "I'm so happy for you, man."

He released Drake, then pulled her into a hug. She stiffened at his arms around her and he released her and stepped back. At his warm smile, she forced a smile onto her own lips. She hoped he didn't think she was standoffish. He was so nice, but when she was close to him, especially when he hugged her, she had to concentrate on stifling the rising feelings of lust within her.

Abel stepped toward her. "Congratulations, Marie."

He offered his hand and she shook it. Tremors tingled along her arm.

"Thank you," she said weakly.

Then they both disappeared out the front entrance. She stared at the closed door.

"I hope they don't think I'm unfriendly."

"Not at all." He stepped close and pulled her into his arms. "Now, just how tired are you?"

When they got to the bedroom, Marie opened her suitcase and pulled out the sexy basque and thong she'd worn the second time she and Drake had made love. She'd intended to put it on for the first time, but they'd gotten so aroused, they'd simply stripped off each other's clothes and gone for it.

Drake headed into the bathroom for a shower and by the time he returned, she was wearing the revealing, red lace outfit. She drank in the sight of him standing there, his broad, muscular chest naked, a white towel draped loosely around his waist.

"I hope you're not too tired." His eyes simmered with heat

as he strode toward her, then he swept her in his arms and kissed her.

She clung to him, allowing all her pent up lust to rush to the surface.

"God, I want you." She stroked down his solid chest. Her fingers brushed against the towel, then she tugged it free.

His cock was already at half-mast. She wrapped her hand around it and stroked, as heat simmered inside her.

"I've missed this monster inside me." She squeezed, then tugged him forward as she backed up to the bed, then sat down and brought his cockhead to her lips.

"It's only been... ah..."—he sucked in a breath as she took him into her mouth—"...a few hours."

She drew his big cockhead from her mouth and smiled. "As I said. Too long."

She licked him like a lollipop, then stretched her lips wide as she swallowed the plum-sized head again. The feel of his hard flesh inside her mouth stoked the flames building within her. She stroked his shaft with her hand as she sucked. Within moments, his cock was rock-hard.

His cock still in her mouth, she glanced up at his face. Suddenly, she imagined that it was Craig standing in front of her, with *his* cock in her mouth. Then Abel stepped up beside her and offered her his cock to suck.

She released Drake's big cock and stood up.

"Come sit down," she said, taking Drake's hand and leading him to the upholstered armchair against the wall near the bed.

He sat down and she sat on his lap, her back to him and his hard cock beneath her. She rocked forward and back, stroking him with her body. Wetness pooled between her legs at the feel of the hard ridge beneath her.

His big hands cupped her breasts and he squeezed and stroked them as she glided forward and back on his erection.

"Damn, sweetheart. That feels so good."

He nuzzled the back of her neck and she reached for his cock and pulled it up between her legs. She leaned back against him as she stroked his cock, enjoying the feel of his hands on her breasts. He slid his fingers under the cups of her bra and tweaked her nipples.

Thoughts of Abel and Craig leaning down in front of her and licking her nipples, then sucking them into their mouths sent a flash frenzy of heightened lust through her. She flicked her clit, imagining it was Drake doing that while his brothers sucked her nipples enthusiastically.

"Oh, Drake. I want you so bad."

His cock twitched in her hand.

"Me too, baby."

Unable to wait a minute longer, she tugged the crotch of her thong aside and lifted her body, then drove down on his huge, solid cock. She gasped as it drove into her.

She loved how it filled her so deeply. He teased her nipple while his other hand slid down her torso, then found her aching clit. He stroked it lightly with his fingertip and she groaned at the intense sensation.

What if Drake lifted her right now and slid into her back opening, then Abel stepped forward with his equally large cock and slid it into her, too.

His finger flicked on her clit again and she moaned.

"Oh, God, I'm so close."

He grasped her hips, lifting, encouraging her to start moving. She moved up, then down, his cock pushing into her again. She felt lightheaded. She pushed herself up again, then dropped down again, moaning at the intense pleasure of his cock stroking her passage. She imagined a cock gliding into her ass, too. The thought sent quivers through her and she moaned.

She bounced up and down, again and again, taking his big

cock deep inside her. Suddenly, bliss blossomed within her, stripping her of conscious thought. She wailed as he guided her hips up and down, continuing her mind-shattering orgasm.

His pelvis jerked upward as a fountain of liquid heat erupted within her. She moaned again at the incredible sensation.

Finally, she collapsed against him, his big cock still inside her.

"Fuck, you are incredible," he murmured in her ear. "I'm so fucking lucky to have found you."

Then he swept her up in his arms, his cock slipping from inside her, and carried her to the bed.

Marie woke up to the sensational feel of warmth between her legs. She gazed down at a male head nuzzling her pussy. Dreams of Craig stroking her body while Abel went down on her still fresh in her sleepy brain, she moaned. "Oh, Abel," she murmured as her fingers twined in his hair.

He gazed up at her. "Abel?"

Jerking wide awake at the sound of Drake's voice, ice water flooded her veins. She cleared her throat.

"Are you *able* to come again so soon?" she said, keeping her voice almost steady.

He prowled over her with a wicked grin. "Just watch me."

He dragged his big cockhead the length of her slick pussy and then teased her opening. When she moaned in frustration, arching against him, he chuckled then drove into her in one hard, deep thrust.

"Oh, God, yes." She clung to him holding him tight to her body. Then he drew back and thrust again.

His big, hard cock glided into her again and again, the thrusts faster and deeper each time.

"Oh, yes." She gulped in breaths of air as his body slammed against hers over and over, pleasure swamping her senses.

"I'm so close, baby." He said each word between thrusts. "How about you?"

She nodded enthusiastically. "Make me come," she pleaded.

He drove in again, with a twist this time, throwing her over the edge of sanity. The orgasm exploded within her, and she gasped.

Still he thrust, driving her pleasure higher and higher. She floated in freefall, enjoying the bliss of a complete departure from physical ties as she floated on a cloud of [sheer] ecstasy.

He groaned and heat filled her, then he collapsed on top of her. She welcomed his weight grounding her as she slowly drifted back from heaven.

He kissed her and rolled to her side, then pulled her against his body. She rested her head against his solid chest, loving the sound of his heartbeat against her ear. Calming. Carrying her back to a deep and pleasant sleep.

Marie woke up and glanced around the strange bedroom. It took a moment for her to realize where she was. This was the master bedroom in Drake's house. *Their* house.

It looked different in the daylight. Bright and spacious, with sunlight streaming in the big windows. Last night in the soft lighting, it had felt close and intimate.

Drake wasn't in bed with her, but she smelled coffee brewing so he was probably downstairs. She glanced at the clock and realized she had just over an hour to get ready for work. Drake said he could drive her and this evening they would go to her place and pick up some of her clothes and her car so she had her own transportation.

She got up and headed for the bathroom. From the damp towel draped over a hook on the door, she could tell Drake had already had his shower. She opened the glass door and stepped inside, then turned on the water, thinking about how nice it would be if Drake stepped into the shower stall with her.

As she ran her soapy hands over her body, her thoughts turned back to last night. The sex between her and Drake had been incredible, better than anything she'd experienced before, but guilt washed through her at the realization that it was because of her hot fantasies of his brothers joining them that had pushed up the intensity.

After her shower, she dried off, then blow dried her hair and put on her makeup. She would arrange to see Lori this weekend and she could tell Lori about all of this. It would be good to talk about it.

Ten minutes later, she walked into the kitchen, dressed and ready for work.

"There's my beautiful bride." Drake, handsome in a gray suit and burgundy tie, gave her a kiss, then guided her to the table. "You sit and I'll bring your breakfast."

He brought her a cup of coffee, then went to the stove and served up a plate of pancakes and bacon, then set it in front of her.

He sat down across the round table from her with his own plate of food. "So I was thinking of having Craig and Abel over tonight for dinner. What do you think?"

She pushed the bacon in front of her with her fork. "Um, maybe not tonight. I'd like to take a little more time to settle in first." She really didn't think she could cope with having them over yet.

He nodded. "Maybe Thursday would work better."

"No, I don't think so. It's a work night and I think it'll be a stressful week with so many changes in our life right now. I really need to get my stuff packed up at home and bring it over here. That's going to take some time."

"I'm sure they'd be happy to help."

She gazed at him. "I'd rather it be just you and me."

He raised an eyebrow. "Okay, then Saturday night."

"Well…"

"Marie, I'm sensing that maybe you don't like my brothers."

She gazed into his concerned blue eyes and felt terrible. She rested her hand on his. "No, Drake, it's nothing like that. I was just hoping we could invite my friend Lori. I have been so looking forward to her meeting you." She squeezed his hand. "You understand, don't you?"

He smiled. "Of course. Invite her over. I'd love to meet her."

She smiled. "Great. You'll love her."

And she would wangle a little time alone with her friend and once she got a chance to discuss her problem with Lori, she was sure Lori would offer some insight and advice that would help her figure this whole thing out.

"Then we'll put a priority on having your brothers over." She smiled. "I really want to get to know them."

And that was the truth. They were Drake's family, so they were very important to her. She wanted to love them just as much as Drake did.

Just not as intimately as her hormones insisted on.

During her lunch break at work, Marie picked up the phone and dialed Lori. She'd sent her an email to let her know she'd gotten back all right and to give her their new address and phone number, but she wanted to talk to her in person.

"Hi," she said when Lori answered the phone.

"Hey, how's married life?"

Marie smiled. "Pretty darned good, actually. I really want you to come and meet Drake. You'll love his house—I mean our house." She giggled. "I really have to get used to that. Anyway, we'd love to have you over for dinner on Saturday."

"I'm afraid I can't."

"Oh. How about Sunday then?"

"No, I can't this weekend."

"Really? Are you sure? I've been looking forward to talking to you. It's been a pretty exciting time and I want to share it with my best friend.

"I'm really sorry."

"Well, maybe we can meet for drinks early next week."

"I don't know. It's pretty busy at work. I really want to see you, but I can't really make any definite plans right now."

"Oh, that's too bad."

"I'm really do want to hear all about how you met Drake and the wedding. Did you get my gift? I mailed it to your apartment."

"No, not yet, but I'll check for it when I go over there to pick up my clothes."

After she hung up, Marie wondered what was going on. She was disappointed that she couldn't talk about her problem with her best friend, but even more she was worried that there was something wrong. Lori didn't sound like herself and she certainly seemed to be avoiding getting together.

Was she jealous of the fact Marie was married now? That wasn't really like Lori, but Marie had heard of other friendships that had faded away after one friend got married.

She really hoped that didn't happen with her and Lori.

"I'm really disappointed she can't come over this weekend," Marie said over dinner.

Drake nodded sympathetically. "Hopefully she can come the following weekend."

Marie pushed the food around her plate. "I don't know. It was like she was avoiding me."

"I think you're just being sensitive. A lot's changed in your life and you want to share it with your friend, but hers is business as usual and if she's busy at work she has to deal with it." He squeezed her hand. "It's the same as you and my brothers. You have a lot to do to get settled in, and I understand that. Otherwise I'd be thinking you were avoiding them." He smiled. "But I know better."

Guilt washed through her and she stared at her dinner.

"But, since we have Saturday free now, how about I invite them over?"

Her stomach clenched and she pushed her dinner aside. He frowned and gazed at her.

"What's wrong?"

She couldn't keep avoiding his brothers without making him think she didn't like them, and she really didn't want him to believe that. But wouldn't telling him the real problem be worse?

"Marie? Is there something wrong?"

She pursed her lips, not sure what to say.

"Marie?"

"About your brothers…"

"Yes?"

"I…" She sucked in a breath, then raised her gaze. Her throat closed up as she tried to find the words."

"You don't want my brothers around?"

"No, it's not that. Exactly. I just…" She wrung her hands together.

"Just tell me, sweetheart."

"I don't know how to say this but… I'm uncomfortable when they're around."

His expression turned stormy. "Did one of them make a pass at you?"

"No. Nothing like that. It's just that… they look so much like you. And sound like you."

He tipped his head. "Yeah. So what are you saying?"

"Well, it's just that…" She frowned. "Well, obviously I'm very attracted to you, and…" She gazed at him again. "As I said, they're so much like you."

"So you're telling me you're attracted to them, and that's what's making you uncomfortable?"

She nodded. He didn't seem angry, which was good.

"So you don't want them around."

"No, it's not that. I just don't know how to handle it. I just need some time to figure it out."

He nodded, but said little over the rest of dinner. He was withdrawn for the rest of the evening and she wondered if he actually was mad. She didn't prod him about it, deciding to give him time to think about it.

The next day, everything seemed back to normal, so she left things alone.

On Saturday afternoon, after they'd finished moving in the last of her things, he gave her a big hug.

"Hey, since we have no plans this evening, I decided to take you out for a romantic evening. How about you put on your sexiest dress, and something black and lacy underneath, then we head out?"

She grinned. "You're on."

~

After they'd had a lovely dinner in a restaurant at the top of the Skyline Hotel overlooking the city lights, Marie walked alongside Drake toward the elevator. When they stepped inside and he pushed the button for floor thirty-one instead of the parking level, she raised an eyebrow.

"I got us a room."

"Really?" she said with a smile.

"I want us to have a romantic evening. Going home to a pile of boxes is definitely not romantic."

She tucked her hand around his arm. "That is true."

The elevator stopped and he led her down the carpeted hallway. At the door, he turned and took her into his arms and kissed her. The heat of his muscular body triggered a different kind of heat in her.

"I want you to stay here for a minute, so I can check something before you come in." He nuzzled her temple. "I want everything to be perfect."

She smiled, remembering the room filled with candles and flowers he'd arranged when they were in Costa Rica.

He slid a keycard in the lock, then opened the door.

"I'll text you when it's time to come in." Then he disappeared into the room, closing the door behind him.

That was odd. Unless...

Would he be waiting for her in bed naked? Her insides quivered. Or maybe he was going to cover strategic places with whipped cream.

A buzzing sounded from her small evening purse. She opened the clasp and checked the message. It was the text from Drake telling her to come in.

She pushed open the door and then sucked in a breath at the sight of three Drakes, devastatingly gorgeous in identical suits and ties, sitting on the bed smiling at her.

Her head spun as she stepped into the room and closed

the door. Candles flickered around the room, setting their handsome smiles aglow.

"What's going on?"

They all stood up and opened their arms to her. Her jaw tightened as she wondered which one was Drake. She walked into the embrace of the Drake on the right and he kissed her, then nuzzled her ear.

"How did you know which was me?"

She just smiled up at him. Thank God she'd picked the right man!

"Now please explain what's going on here," she said.

"You said you were attracted to my brothers and I thought"—his eyes glittered—"that maybe you'd like to act on that attraction."

Her eyes widened and her heartbeat accelerated. "Are you serious?"

"I want to do something to help you get past your awkwardness with my brothers."

"By having me sleep with..." She gazed at the Drake beside her.

"Abel," he offered.

"And me," the other Drake said with a wide grin.

She turned to Drake. "You want me to sleep with both of them?" Both shock and excitement quivered through her.

"I think the idea turns you on." Drake stepped toward her with a devilish smile. "And that turns me on."

"And it definitely turns us on," said Craig while Abel nodded in agreement.

Marie's stomach fluttered at the sight of the three identical men smiling at her with twinkles in their eyes.

She turned her gaze to Drake. "And you won't be jealous."

"As long as I know your heart is mine, that's all that matters."

"It is." She stepped into his arms and kissed him passionately.

He held her tight to his strong body and she melted against him.

"Um… if you two really want to be alone, we can call it a night."

Marie drew back and smiled at Drake, then turned and grabbed the lapels of Abel's suit and pulled him close.

"Not on you life." She meshed her lips with his.

He wrapped his arms around her and devoured her mouth.

Craig stepped behind her and his hands stroked over her shoulders, then his lips nuzzled her neck. He pressed closer and she was sandwiched between the two hot, hard bodies. Muscular and solid.

Just like Drake.

Craig's hands glided down, grazing the sides of her breasts, then he grasped her hips and drew her back against him. The big bulge in his pants pressed hard against her ass. His hands glided over her breasts and he cupped them in his big hands. She pulled her mouth from Abel's and sucked in a deep breath.

Abel grasped her hips and pressed against her, the bulge of his erection pushing against her belly.

Oh, God, two big cocks, hard and ready for her.

She glanced toward Drake, watching the three of them, his hand gliding over his crotch.

"Oh, baby, bring it out so I can see it," she said.

She watched with longing as he unzipped his trousers, then drew out his big, long, familiar cock. She smiled and licked her lips, then gazed up at Abel.

"Now I want to see yours." She reached around behind her and stroked along Craig's thigh, then over his swelling cock. "Yours, too."

Abel stepped back and unzipped his pants, then dropped them to the floor, followed by his navy boxers. Her gaze locked on his big, solid cock, red and throbbing, as he wrapped his hand around it and stroked. She smiled and turned toward Craig, who still stood close to her body. She sank to her knees and unzipped his pants, then reached inside.

Oh, God, it was hot and hard. She ran her fingertips over the kid-leather soft skin, then wrapped her fingers around it. Rock solid and pulsing in her hand. She brought it to her mouth and wrapped her lips around it. So big, she had to stretch. But she was used to that with Drake.

Abel stepped behind her and stroked her back, then slipped the straps of her dress off her shoulders. He then crouched down and guided it down her body until it pooled around her knees.

She couldn't believe she had this big cock in her mouth— not her husband's—and another man was undressing her. Craig's fingers slid through her hair as she glided deeper on his long cock.

"Sweetheart, that feels so good."

Abel's fingers worked at the hooks of her bra, and it released, then he stripped it away. At the cool air surrounding her nipples, they hardened and thrust forward. Abel ran his fingertips over them and she murmured around the hard flesh in her mouth.

She began to suck Craig in earnest, gliding her mouth up and down on him as Abel teased her nipples, sending fiery heat blazing along her nerve endings. She tucked her hands under his balls, fondling them as she surged on his cock.

"Oh, God, woman." He groaned, then jerked forward, spurting hot liquid into her mouth.

She continued sucking, then swallowed and sucked some more, until he finally had no more.

His cock slid from her mouth and he drew her to her feet and kissed her, then scooped her up and carried her to one of the armchairs. He sat down, pulling her onto his lap. Abel crouched in front of them and stroked her naked breasts.

"Man, brother, you have excellent taste in women," Abel said to Drake without ever taking his gaze from her breasts.

She leaned back against Craig. "Take them in your mouth," she pleaded.

Abel leaned forward and licked her nipple, sending wild sensations surging through her. Then he covered it with his lips and sucked.

"Oh, God, yes."

Craig ran his hand over her other nipple, then squeezed the bud between his fingertips. Heat throbbed through her.

"Abel, take off her panties." Drake said. "I bet she's soaking wet."

Abel tucked his fingers under the elastic of her thong, then drew it down her legs. He tossed it aside and Craig stroked up her thigh. She sucked in a breath as his big fingers stroked over her slick folds. Abel pressed her knees apart and stared at his brother's fingers gliding over her. Then one of those big fingers slid inside her and she moaned.

"You're right, Drake. She's dripping wet and ready."

Abel stood in front of her and pressed his cock to her lips as Craig glided another finger inside her. She opened and Abel filled her mouth with cock. Big and thick. Gliding deep into her mouth.

She gasped as Craig glided his fingers in an out, and she squeezed him, then began to suck on Abel.

"Oh, yeah, honey." Abel surged forward and back.

She tried to suck, but the feel of Craig's fingers fucking her gently distracted her. Heedless, Abel fucked her mouth with gentle, but deep strokes of his cock.

"Damn, this is so fucking sexy." Drake shed his shirt and pants and stroked his big cock while he watched.

"Damn, your mouth is so fucking warm. I could shoot my load right now."

"Why don't you do it, Abel? Fill my wife's mouth with your cum."

Drake's coarse, dirty words, filled her with excitement. She squeezed Abel's big cock in her mouth. He cupped her head, as he glided in and out. Faster. She sucked and he groaned.

"Come on. Fuck my wife's sexy mouth."

Craig, clearly just as turned on as the rest of them, judging by his swollen member pressing into her backside, glided his fingers into her faster.

She grabbed Abel's balls and stroked them as she sucked him harder.

"Oh, fuck." Abel groaned and shuddered against her.

Her mouth filled with liquid heat again. He pulled away, his cock falling from her lips, but then he crouched down and took her nipple back into his mouth, cupping her other breast with his hand.

Craig's fingers continued to thrust inside her and the heat surging through her blossomed into intense pleasure that wafted through her in waves.

"Oh, God, I'm…" She gasped for air as bliss exploded within her, and she threw her head back and moaned.

Abel leaned down and licked her clit, sending her pleasure even higher. She clung to his head forcing his mouth tighter to her, as his brother's fingers continued to plunge in and out.

Finally, the waves subsided and she collapsed against Craig. He stroked her hair back from her face and kissed her temple.

"You know we've only just begun, right."

She gazed dreamily at the three identical men in front of her and sighed.

"I can't believe I'm so lucky. You are all so sexy."

Craig laughed and kissed the top of her head. "I think we're the lucky ones."

His cock, now fully hard again, was a hard bulge against her backside. She could just wiggle and shift a little and he would glide into her. Oh, God she wanted to feel his big cock inside her. And Abel's. *And* Drake's.

She gazed over at her husband.

"Come here, Drake."

"You look occupied right now, and I'm loving the show."

"The show will go on, but you haven't come yet." She stretched her open hand toward him. "Let me help you."

He stood and walked toward her, his enormous, sexy cock bouncing. She wrapped her hand around it, loving the hot, hard feel of it, and stroked. She stood up and bent forward, wrapped her lips around his bulbous cockhead, her legs wide, leaving her backside open and available to Craig.

Craig leaned forward and she felt his tongue nudge her slick flesh. She drove down hard on Drake. Craig wrapped his hands around her thighs and licked her. She moaned around Drake's cock. Her fingers tightened around him as she slid up and down his shaft. His fingers glided through her hair, drawing it back from her face.

"I love watching you do that," he said with a smile.

"Fuck, me too," Abel said, his hand gliding up and down his own hard cock.

She reached out her hand to him and drew her mouth off Drake briefly. "Here," she said, then dove down on Drake again.

Craig licked her again and she groaned. Abel approached her and she wrapped her hand around him and began to stroke. She glided on Drake a couple more times.

Craig's tongue gently nudged her opening, then pushed inside.

She slipped off the end. "Oh, yes."

Craig's tongue swirled inside her, then slid out again.

"Closer," she said to Abel, drawing him forward with a gentle pull on his member.

He stepped beside Drake and she covered Abel with her mouth. She'd already brought him to orgasm once, but it was so sexy and wildly naughty to shift from one big cock to another. She sucked Abel, then returned to Drake, his big cock filling her again. After a few seconds, she switched back to Abel.

Craig stroked her slick folds with his fingers, then his tongue found her clit. She tightened her hold on Drake and bobbed up and down on him faster.

"God, sweetheart, I'm going to come."

"Mmm." She slid away, stroking him vigorously, her other hand stroking Abel.

"Oh, God, me too." She took him deep again as Craig fluttered his tongue on her sensitive button.

Drake moaned, then jerked forward, filling her mouth with cum. She sucked and swallowed, then he dropped from her mouth as she gasped at the feel of Craig's fingertip brushing her clit. The intense pleasure spiked through her and she groaned.

"God, you're coming again." Abel groaned and spurted hot, white liquid onto her arm, then it dribbled down her fingers as the continuing flow glazed his solid cock.

She tightened her hold on him, still stroking, as she continued to ride the wave of pleasure Craig was giving her with his intimate touch.

Drake crouched down and cupped her hanging breasts in his big, warm hands, then squeezed and stroked, driving her pleasure higher. Abel's cock slipped from her fingers and he stroked her behind. Craig sucked on her clit and she wailed louder, shooting to ecstatic heights.

All the erotic sensations bombarding her blended into one blissful whole and she groaned, letting herself go to it.

Finally, the pleasure waned, replaced by a deep sense of satisfaction. She stood up and stepped forward with shaky legs. Drake scooped her up and set her on the bed, gazing down at her with an indulgent smile.

"Guys, I really think my wife needs to be fucked now."

Craig grinned. "It's a tough job, but someone's got to do it."

He stepped forward, his big cock bobbing up and down, and he prowled over her. She opened her arms to him, longing for that monster to impale her.

Craig grasped his cock and stroked her slick folds with the tip.

"Are you ready for me?" he asked.

"You can feel that I am," she murmured, stroking his hair from his face. "Drive your big cock into me," she pleaded.

"Fuck, yeah." He drove forward, filling her with one long thrust.

"Oh, God, you're so big." She clung to his shoulders. "Please fuck me."

"Wait," Drake said firmly.

She glanced at him. Had he changed his mind?

"Sweetheart, aren't you forgetting about Abel?" Drake asked.

She glanced at Abel, who stood beside the bed stroking his cock, which amazingly was hard again.

"I… uh…"

Craig wrapped his arms around her and rolled over, shifting her on top of him. Abel stepped behind her and grasped her hips, then lifted them.

"You want both of us inside you at the same time, don't you?"

She quivered at the thought.

"Oh, God, yes."

Drake handed Abel a tube of lube and a moment later she felt his slick fingers glide into her anal opening. First one, then two. He stretched and stroked her for several moments. She clenched around Craig's big cock, wildly turned on.

Then she felt something bigger nudge her back opening and Abel slowly pressed his cockhead into her. Patiently. Filling her slowly. Once his cockhead filled her, he stopped for a moment, then soon pushed deeper.

"I love watching Abel's big cock fill your ass," Drake said.

"And I love having my big cock inside your wife's pussy," Craig said.

"And I love everything about this whole thing," Abel said, as his cock slid in the rest of the way.

"Oh, God, I can't believe I have two big cocks inside me." The bulging erections throbbed within her. She gazed over at Drake, his cock jutting forward like a rigid spear.

"Come for us, sweetheart. Let us watch you writhe in ecstasy."

"Oh, yes. Please fuck me."

The two brother's started to move, their members drawing back, then driving forward again. The feel of the two hard bodies surrounding her, the thick shaft moving inside her, overwhelmed her. She moaned, then arched against Craig, taking him deeper.

The men found a rhythm and she loved the feel of the two cocks stroking her insides, driving her pleasure higher.

"How does it feel, sweetheart?" Drake asked.

"Oh, God it's…" she moaned. The thrumming in her body intensified. "It's so incredible."

Abel kissed her shoulder and the gentle touch sent her

spiraling out of control. The cocks filled her again and again and she moaned as pleasure skyrocketed through her, building to swirling heights, blasting through her body in a massive swell of bliss.

Then she catapulted to heaven, clinging to Craig's shoulders as both men continued to drive into her. She wailed loud and long, riding the wave of ecstasy.

Craig's hips jerked upward, a fountain of heat filling her, then Abel groaned his release. The three of them shuddered in sheer pleasure, then collapsed together in a heap.

Abel rolled off her and stretched out on the bed, a huge smile on his face, then she rolled to the other side, flopping beside Craig. She raked her hand through her long hair, completely sated.

"That was the most incredible experience I've ever had." Her wide smile stretched her face as she lay there happily.

"I think it's my turn now." Drake moved toward the bed purposefully.

His brothers slipped from the bed as Drake prowled over her. His big, powerful cock brushed her stomach, then he grasped it and pressed it to her wet opening.

"I love you, Marie."

He drove forward, impaling her. Her arms wrapped around him and she arched forward.

"I love you, too, Drake. Now please fuck me."

He glided back, then drove forward again. His lips nuzzled her neck as he thrust into her again and again. She squeezed him tight inside her, feeling the pleasure rise inside her.

"Oh, I'm so close." She clung to his shoulders.

"Me, too."

His big cock drove deep and she moaned as another orgasm blasted through her.

"I'm coming," she murmured breathlessly, then wailed as he drove deep again.

"Fuck, yes." He arched against her and shuddered as he erupted inside her.

She squeezed him intimately, riding the wave of ecstasy yet again.

Finally, they collapsed together, holding each other close. He kissed her forehead, then his lips found hers and the kiss turned passionate.

"I am a lucky man."

She rested her head against his chest and smiled.

"I guess we should leave you two alone," Craig said.

Craig and Abel headed for the adjoining door.

"Are you kidding?" Drake said. "The night is still young."

Marie laughed. When she married Drake she'd known she was the luckiest woman in the world.

Little did she know then just how lucky she was.

THREE SECRETS

Now are you ready for Abel's happy ending?

Keeping one secret is intriguing.
Two is naughty.
Three... deserves to be punished.
Sharing secrets has never been so exhilarating...

Nicole's heart clenched when she saw Abel sitting across the park on the wooden bench, the sunlight shimmering on his wavy, dark brown hair. He looked just like she remembered him when she'd first seen him in Paris.

She'd fallen in love with him ten minutes after she'd met him.

But after spending two months together traveling around Europe, she'd realized with an aching heart that the sweet, gentle-spirited man he was would not really understand her, or accept her... idiosyncrasies.

So, even though it was the most painful thing she'd ever done, she'd walked away. When they'd returned to Canada, she'd gone home to Edmonton to let their relationship die.

At least, that's what she'd intended. But it had been too difficult to stay away.

He glanced up and she knew the moment he spotted her. His eyes lit up and his smile, so bright and cheerful, set his face aglow. Warmth washed through her at the sight. He stood up and stepped forward—one step, then another—until he was racing toward her. She blinked back tears of joy as he flung his arms around her and spun her in a circle. When she felt the ground beneath her feet again, his lips found hers and his tongue swept into her mouth, singeing her senses.

Oh, God, how had she survived so long without him?

Her arms came around him and she melted into the passion of his kiss.

"Nicole, I can't believe you're here." He gazed at her, his lips turned up in a dazzling smile. "It seems like forever since we've seen each other."

She laughed, joy bubbling through her. "It's only been three months."

His face turned serious. "I'd begun to worry I'd never see you again." He hesitated, as if he wanted to say more—probably ask her why she hadn't responded to his repeated attempts to contact her—but instead he took her hand and squeezed it. "I'm really looking forward to getting re-acquainted."

From the glimmer in his eyes, hot images of the two of them entwined on a bed naked, their bodies joined intimately, sent heat washing through her. She wanted that so badly.

It would be so easy to just go with him right now. To lose herself in his loving arms. But she couldn't do that until she told him her secret.

"Let's sit down and talk first," she said.

His eyebrows arched. "Talk. Really?" His hand stroked over her shoulder possessively and he leaned in close, his warmth seeping into her. "I can think of much more interesting things to do than talk," he murmured against her ear, the warmth of his breath sending a quiver through her.

But she steeled herself, staying strong. "Yes, really. Talk."

She tugged on his hand as she led him to the bench, then sat down, apprehension building inside her. He settled beside her.

"What is it you want to talk about?" he asked.

She pursed her lips and he frowned.

"Why am I getting the feeling you didn't meet me to continue our relationship after all?" He took both her hands and held them tight. "You know I'm crazy about you. I thought we had a real chance at making things work between us. Don't you want that?"

Her breath caught. "Of course I do," she said, her voice a mere whisper. It was what she wanted more than anything in the world. She drew her hand free and stroked his cheek, loving the raspy, masculine feel of his light stubble.

His smile returned and her throat closed up.

"But the question is will you still want me after I tell you what I came here to say?"

Abel stared at Nicole, the woman he hadn't stopped thinking about since he'd left Europe. It had been ironic, since his trip had been partly to escape the help of his brothers and their new wives who had been driving him crazy trying to play matchmaker, wanting him to find the same happiness they had found. Who knew he would stumble across the woman of his dreams in a park in Paris?

They had spent two wonderful months together, and as it came close to time to return home, he'd known he should tell Nicole his secret, but he was afraid it would scare her away for good. After all, how did he tell a sweet, girl-next-door type like Nicole that *hey, my brothers and I are into sharing women.*

He had already indulged in sexual adventures with both his brothers' wives and he'd had many a dream about sharing Nicole with them, with or without their wives, though images of Nicole going down on Marie sent almost painful need slicing through him.

He was sure it would never happen, though. It might be some women's fantasy, but he was sure Nicole would disapprove. She seemed so... straight-laced.

But even though he hadn't told her his secret, she had seemed reluctant to continue their relationship once they returned home. When he hadn't heard from her after so many months, he thought he'd lost her for good.

Then he'd gotten her email last week and hope had soared within him.

Now it seemed she had a secret, too.

She gazed at him, her blue eyes wide. "This might come as a shock to you but… I'm not what you think I am."

He grinned and arched his eyebrows. "Are you a dude?"

But her expression remained serious. "This is really hard." She stroked his cheek again, her gentle touch sending shimmers of heat through him. "I love the way you look at me and I'm afraid that after I tell you, that look will… change."

He took her hand and squeezed. "I don't think that's possible, but go ahead and tell me." At her continued hesitation, he said, "Just take a deep breath and do it."

He watched her chest rise and fall as she took his advice, then she gazed down at their joined hands.

"You think of me as sweet and a little naïve, but that's far from the truth. When you and I have sex it's tender and passionate and lovely. Everything a woman would want."

He smiled, delighting in her praise.

"At least, most women."

Fuck, was she going to tell him he wasn't good enough in bed?

"So what am I doing wrong?"

Her eyes widened. "No, it's not you. It's me."

"Ah, classic break up line."

"Abel, this is serious."

"I know, sweetheart. Just tell me."

"Okay. I'm into BDSM."

He didn't know what he'd expected, but it wasn't that.

"So you want to be tied up? Or you want me to dominate you?"

"Well, no. Actually…"

~

"She's a Domme." Abel picked up the burger Marie, Drake's wife, set in front of him and bit into it.

"A Domme?" Drake's eyes twinkled. "So does she have whips and chains?"

Abel shrugged. "I don't know." He grinned. "But I'd sure like to find out."

"I can't help envisioning a full latex suit with spike heeled boots," said Drake. "And a whip."

Marie grinned at him. "Are you trying to tell me something? Does someone want to submit to the control of his woman?"

Across the table, their other brother, Craig, raised his hand. Drake also put his hand in the air.

Abel laughed. "Well, girls, maybe you can take lessons from Nicole."

Lori smiled. "That could be fun."

"So you and Nicole are together again?" Marie asked.

"No."

Marie's eyes widened. "No?"

"Well, not yet. I told her I needed to think about things."

"Why?" Lori asked.

"Well, she seemed so convinced that I might need time to get used to the idea that I didn't want to disappoint her."

Marie shook her head. "That just sounds mean."

"Not at all. It gives her a chance to try and convince me. And more importantly, it gives me a chance to ask a few questions to find out if she's okay with my secret. Not every woman is okay with a man sharing her with his two brothers."

Lori giggled. "Though for the life of me, I can't understand why."

"When are you going to see her again?" Craig asked.

"I've arranged to meet her at her hotel tomorrow night."

~

Nicole was worried.

She hadn't known exactly what to expect when she told Abel about her being a Domme, and at least he hadn't outright rejected her, but he hadn't accepted the idea with open arms, either. He'd seemed cautiously curious and had suggested they talk about it when they had more time and could go somewhere private. So she'd invited him to her hotel.

A knock sounded on the door.

She stood up and approached the door. She loved him and she was determined to convince him they should be together, so she would do everything she could to persuade him. When she peered through the peephole, her heart swelled at the sight of his familiar, handsome face.

She opened the door. "Come in."

She wanted to throw her arms around him and kiss him, to feel his hard body against hers, but instead she turned and walked into the room. She wore a black leather skirt and a silk shirt that fluttered as she walked. Although loose fitting, the shirt draped nicely and silhouetted her curves in a flattering manner. She could almost feel the heat of his gaze on her ass as he followed her. She sat down in the upholstered chair by the low table she'd pulled into the center of the room and gestured for him to sit in the desk chair she'd placed facing hers.

"Thank you for coming. I'll answer any questions you want."

He nodded. "Good."

His expression was serious and she worried he'd already made up his mind and had just come here out of courtesy.

He leaned back in the chair. "So, you're a Domme. I'm not really sure what that means, but I am curious about one thing. Do you do it with a lot of different men?"

Her stomach tightened. Did he think she did it professionally?

"I wouldn't say a lot of men. Just the ones I've had a sexual relationship with."

She realized that didn't really answer the question, but he didn't press it further.

"I'm curious if you've dominated more than one man at a time," he said.

Her lips compressed. "That's like me asking if you've had a threesome with two women."

"That's true. I guess I'm just curious how adventurous you are with sex."

She raised an eyebrow. "How about we focus on the fact I'm a Domme, so I can address your concerns?"

He nodded. "Okay, why don't you just explain to me what you do?"

"That's a pretty broad question, but I'll do my best." Now was the time to put her skills to work. "But first, there's a bottle of water in the fridge, and a clean glass and a bucket of ice on the counter. I'd like some ice water. Would you mind?"

"Sure." He stood up and fetched the water, then set the tinkling glass on the table in front of her.

She took a sip and set it down again.

"So as a Domme, I take control of the situation. This can be only in the bedroom, or beyond that if that's what my partner wants."

"You never did that with us," he said.

"No. I didn't want to scare you away. Our romance started fast and because of circumstances, I knew we wouldn't be together long. With previous lovers, I had the luxury of time to build a relationship and introduce the domination slowly." She gazed into his blue eyes, willing him to understand. "You were so special and I wanted it to work between us so badly...

I tried to ignore my usual tendency to take control. I did it, but it was a struggle, and I realized I was denying who I really am, and a relationship cannot continue if it requires that."

He nodded. "I understand."

She picked up the water, the ice cubes clinking against the side of the glass, and took another sip. "I don't know about you, but I find it hot in here." In fact, she'd turned up the heat so it was a little warm. "Would you turn down the thermostat?"

As he walked to the control box on the wall, she unfastened the sash on her shirt and released the two buttons holding it closed, then dropped the garment from her shoulders and laid it over the arm of the chair. Underneath she wore a snug, black leather top with a zipper down the front and a zipper slashing across each breast.

When he sat back down, his gaze dropped to the silver zipper over her left breast. She fanned herself with her hand and drew the front zipper down a little, revealing cleavage. His gaze followed her movement, his eyes glittering. She dragged her fingertips along her skin as she drew her hand away.

"That's an interesting top. Are you planning to pull out the whips and chains and dominate me right now?"

She smiled. "I think you'd like me to chain you up so you're helpless, then take advantage of you," she said in a seductive voice. Actually, she had no idea and said it just to see his reaction. His expression remained closed, but she could see his cock getting hard beneath the denim.

So, he was interested.

"But to answer your question, I'm not planning anything so brute force. I do think it's a good idea to give you a taste of what I do, though."

He leaned back, crossing his arms over his chest. "All right. Go ahead."

She smiled. "I've already started."

He tipped his head. "What do you mean?"

"You've already performed two tasks for me. And I've found out that you are open to the idea of being chained up. At least, that's what the bulge in your pants tells me."

He compressed his lips. "Okay, so you're going to give me a demonstration?"

"Will you be open to it?"

He nodded. "Sure. So what do you want me to do?"

"First, you ask no more questions. You just do as you're told." She'd added an authoritative edge to her voice, but not too much. She wanted to ease him into this. "Do you understand?"

"Yes."

"When you address me, call me Ma'am or Mistress."

"Yes, Ma'am."

She smiled. "Very good. Now first I want to make it clear that we will not be having sex tonight. I am just going to give you a taste of what it's like to be dominated by me."

She sipped her water, then leaned back in her chair, crossed her legs, which she knew gave him a great view of her thighs, and stared at him speculatively.

"That cock looks uncomfortable bound up in all that fabric. Unzip and take it out."

Keeping a disinterested expression, she watched with hunger as he dragged down the zipper and reached under the denim. Her insides heated as he pulled his big, hard cock into view.

It was hard as rock and the veins along the sides pulsed in his hand.

"Move your hand away and don't touch it again until I give you permission. I want to look at it."

"Yes, Ma'am."

He moved his hand away and she drank in the site of the

big, bulbous tip, then slid her gaze downward to the base. It twitched under her scrutiny, growing even harder.

"I like it. It's big and hard." She uncrossed her legs, spreading her knees as much as her tight leather skirt would allow. This gave him a view up her skirt to the crotch of the tiny red lace panties underneath.

"Are you looking up my skirt?" she said with an edge to her voice, but bit back the word slave. It would be too much right now.

His gaze flicked from her crotch to her face.

"Ordinarily, I would punish you for that, but since this is new to you, I'll let you off with a warning. You only look at my body if I give you permission. Understand?"

"Yes, Mistress."

"Good. I think you deserve a reward." She grasped the tag of the zipper on the front of her skirt at the hem, and drew it upward, revealing her naked thighs. As the leather parted, she widened her legs, knowing he'd be able to see her skimpy, red panties. She stopped a few inches below the waist. She stroked her inner thigh. "Do you like what you see?"He nodded, his eyes locked on the crotch of her panties.

"Good. I admit the sight of that big cock of yours, so hard from wanting me, is turning me on." She slid her fingertip over the panties, feeling the wetness soaking the fabric. God, she wanted so badly to feel that big cock of his inside her again. But she had to be firm with herself and leave him wanting more.

She ran her hands up her torso, over the leather of her top, then cupped both her breasts. She undid one of the zippers, then parted the leather, revealing her naked breast.

His hand moved to his cock and wrapped around it.

"I said don't touch your cock."

Her commanding voice startled him and he released his

shaft. He grasped the armrests on the chair, his fingers curling around them.

She stroked her nipple, which tightened immediately. "Come over here."

He stood up and approached her, his gaze locked on her fingers as she caressed the hard bud. Tingles danced through her and she longed for his touch.

"Kneel down in front of me." She waited while he complied. The feel of him so close... the heat of his big masculine body... sent her hormones dancing.

She dropped her hands to her sides. "Now touch me."

His big hand moved toward her and he touched her hard nipple. Pleasure burst through her and she stifled a gasp. He stroked over the tip, then pinched it between his fingertips.

"The other one, too." Try as she did to keep a flat tone, there was a roughness to her voice.

He touched her other nipple, then pinched it, too. First one, then the other. Then both at the same time. Heat washed through her.

"If you want to take one in your mouth, you may."

Immediately, he leaned forward and she couldn't stop her moan at the feel of his hot mouth surrounding her. Then he began to suck.

Oh, God, much more of this and she'd be begging him to fuck her.

"Stop."

He took another suck, then slowly released her from his mouth. If he'd been a more experienced sub, and she hadn't been trying to woo him, she'd have punished him for that.

"Stand up."

Once he stood up, his erection was right in front of her face. It was big, hard as steel, and in need of release. Her insides tightened and she longed to demand he thrust it inside her and satisfy her intense craving for him. She wanted to feel his hard body against her as he drove deep into her, then thrust again and again until she wept in pleasure.

Damn, she should just say the session was over and send him away right now, leaving him wanting more, but if she didn't do something about that swollen cock immediately, her will power would surely slip. And she couldn't quite bring herself to leave him like this.

"You've been very good, so I'm going to reward you."

She wrapped her hand around his cock and stroked, then she brought it to her lips and licked him. Salty precum tingled across her tongue. She opened wide and drew him inside.

To her delight, he groaned. She glided down on him, taking his long shaft as deep as she could. Then she slid back. She dove down again and slid back, then off the tip.

"I give you permission to come," she said, then took him deep again.

His hand cupped her head, his fingers coiling in her hair.

"Yes, Mistress." The words, uttered with such need, thrilled her.

She bobbed up and down, squeezing him in her mouth. She stroked his balls, feeling them harden, and as she moved faster, she felt him stiffen. Then he groaned and hot liquid erupted from his cock, filling her mouth and driving her need higher. She kept sucking him, until he had no more to give.

Slowly, she slid away, releasing his cock reluctantly, trying to ignore the intense ache inside her.

She gazed up at him, his face flushed, his breathing heavy, and smiled.

"So do you have a better idea of what I do?"

He nodded and zipped up his pants, looking a little dazed.

"I think I'd better go." To her surprise, he grabbed his jacket and headed to the door. "Good night."

The door closed after him and she just stared at it in shock.

~

Abel closed the door behind him, then strode down the hall to the elevator in a daze. Damn, that was the most intense sexual experience he'd ever had. She was so fucking hot!

She'd said they wouldn't have sex tonight, but if he'd stayed, he wouldn't have been able to help himself. The memory of her swollen nipple in his mouth, his tongue swirling over the hard bud, had him growing hard again. If he'd stayed another moment, his intense desire to see her lovely face glowing in orgasm would have driven him to try and seduce her into letting him enter her hot, sweet pussy. In order to respect her wishes, he'd needed to get out of there fast.

He hadn't succeeded in finding out if she'd be open to a foursome with his brothers. Of course, he hadn't. His focus had been totally blown.

Fuck, he couldn't stop thinking of her hot lips around him, gliding up and down his cock. Damn, he was already hard as a rock again. He wanted to fly back to her room and beg her to let him fuck her.

But he wanted to play the game a little longer. Keep her wondering.

And he still had to figure out how to reveal his secret without scaring her away.

~

The next morning, when Nicole returned to her room after

breakfast, there was a message waiting for her. She smiled. Maybe it was from Abel.

She picked up the receiver and dialed the number to retrieve her messages.

"Hello, Nicole. I think we should meet one more time. Please come to 25 Losagos Drive at 7 p.m. tonight. You've told me your secret and I must admit I have a secret of my own I'd like to share with you before you go."

Her chest clenched. He wanted to see her *one more time*. That sounded like he wanted to say good-bye.

He also said he had a secret, too. That peaked her curiosity, but not enough to draw her attention from the fact she didn't want to lose him. She would meet him this evening and do everything she could to convince him they should be together, even if it meant suppressing her need to take control. She cursed herself. Why had she taken the chance on losing him by admitting it in the first place? She could have kept her secret hidden.

She sighed. But, no. It was better that he knew. Maybe he would be willing to give a relationship with her a try if she promised to do her best to block her natural tendency to dominate.

What was Abel's secret? The question had been swirling around Nicole's mind all afternoon.

She left the hotel and flagged down a cab.

About twenty minutes later, the cab pulled up in front of a lovely inn on the outskirts of the city. It wasn't what Nicole had expected. If he was going to break up with her, she would have thought he'd just pick a restaurant in the city to keep it simple.

She went inside and glanced around. She didn't see him, so she walked to reception.

"I'm supposed to meet someone here. My name's Nicole Justin. Is there a message?"

The young woman tapped at her computer screen, then smiled. "Yes, Ms. Justin. Mr. Carter is in room 512 and asked that we give you a key." The woman handed her a key card, then directed her to the elevators.

He'd gotten a room? Her lips turned up in a smile as she got on the elevator and pushed the button for the fifth floor. The doors whooshed closed. Leaving him wanting more had definitely worked. Her heart thumped loudly in anticipation. She wanted to be with him again. To feel his hands skimming over her body, then explore her intimate places.

The doors opened and she walked down the hall. But maybe he just wanted to talk somewhere private. What was this secret of his?

She stopped in front of a double door. Room 512.

She slipped the keycard in the slot and opened the door, then stepped into a large tiled entrance lit by an elegant table-top lamp. To her left was what looked like a change room, with a counter and a huge mirror, attached to a bathroom. Beyond she could see a sitting area with a couch and chairs. He'd gotten a suite.

She stepped into the room and glanced around.

"Hello, Mistress."

Her breath caught at the sight of Abel, wearing only tight, black briefs, standing against a stripper pole, his hands behind his back. She glanced to the ceiling and saw that it was one of the portable poles held in place with pressure rather than being bolted to the floor and ceiling.

"Hello. What's this all about?"

"I told you I have a secret, and once I tell you what it is, I think you'll want to punish me."

Excitement skittered through her. Thoughts of punishing him in all kinds of ways raced through her brain. Did this mean he accepted her lifestyle?

She stepped into the room, wishing she'd worn something black and leather. She walked around behind him and excitement danced through her at the sight of his wrists fastened together around the pole with handcuffs.

She suppressed a smile.

"If I'm going to punish you, I'll need tools. I don't want to hurt my hand spanking that tight ass of yours." She glanced around, wondering what she could make use of in the room. There was a dining room in the suite, but not a kitchen, which might have had a wooden spoon.

"Yes, Mistress. If you look in the drawer by the TV you'll see I brought some things."

She walked to the drawer and opened it. Inside was a selection of floggers, a wooden paddle, and a riding crop. She picked up the crop and ran her fingers over the heart-shaped leather on the tip. She would love to use this and leave red, heart shapes all over his sexy ass, but it would be too much for their first time. Instead, she picked up the soft, baby-blue suede flogger and placed it on top of the dresser. There were also garments in the drawer. She picked up one of the black leather straps and lifted it. It was a harness that would cover very little of her body, but had a triangle of leather over the crotch and a strip to cover each breast. There were also black spike heels. She checked and they were her size.

She grasped the harness and walked in front of him, then held it up. "Do you expect me to wear this?" she demanded sternly.

He bowed his head. "Only if it pleases you, Mistress."

She allowed a slow smile to spread across her face. "It does."

She went back to the drawer and grabbed the shoes and

flogger, then strode from the room to the change room by the front door and flung off her clothes, then pulled on the sexy harness and high heels. She returned to the living area with the flogger in her hand, feeling every bit the Dominatrix.

His gaze locked on her and his dark blue eyes grew heated. She could see the black fabric of his briefs grow tight over his bulge.

She pretended to pay attention to the flogger, enjoying a few seconds of his admiration, then glanced at him.

"Eyes down," she commanded.

He complied and she walked closer.

"Did you like what you saw?" she asked as she walked around him, taking in the sexy sight of his big, muscular body. Knowing he was ready to obey her every command sent heat simmering through her.

"Yes, Ma'am."

"Good. You may raise your eyes again."

He gazed at her, excitement glimmering in his eyes. She pressed the end of the flogger lightly against his stomach, then dragged it upward, the long strands dragging along his torso.

"You said you have a secret. What is it?"

He hesitated and she narrowed her eyes. "When I give you a command, I expect you to comply immediately. Understand?"

"Yes, Ma'am. It's about my brothers. As you know, I'm a triplet."

She nodded.

"The secret is that my brothers and I sometimes... uh... share women."

"Share? In what way?" She knew in exactly what way, and excitement shot through her at the idea, but she wanted him to confirm it.

"Sexually. All three of us would make love to a woman at the same time."

Abel was exceptionally hunky. The thought of two more men just like him touching her, sandwiching her between them… fucking her. God, that was hot.

"Tell me more."

"Like what?" he asked.

"How do three of you have sex with a woman at the same time?"

"Sometimes we alternate… uh… penetrating her. Sometimes one of us is in front and the other behind."

Her insides tightened in need.

"What about the third brother?"

"Well, one time, two of us… uh…"

"Fucked?"

His glance darted to her and he smiled. "Yes, two of us fucked one woman while another woman kept our third brother busy."

"Really? Then that's not really three men with one woman."

But, God, it was so hot that they did it with more than one woman.

"Another time when two of us were inside a woman," he continued, "she gave oral sex to our brother." His smooth tone told her he knew this was turning her on. And, damn, was it ever.

She smiled. "Well, don't expect that from me. If I have two, or three of you fucking me, I want to focus on enjoying it."

His eyes lit up. "You mean, you'd consider—"

"Silence. I ask the questions, not you."

His expression turned subdued. "Yes, Mistress."

"Well, you're right. You should definitely be punished."

She dragged the flogger around his ribs as she walked

behind him, then she drew it back and gazed at the black cotton covering him. To do this properly, she'd have to turn him around, or move him somewhere he could bend over, displaying his fine ass to her. And, of course, he'd have to get rid of those briefs. She wanted to see his naked buttocks clenching as she whipped them.

She drew in a deep breath. *Easy now.* She didn't want to go too far.

To move him, she'd have to uncuff him and she rather liked having him restrained.

She pressed her finger to his back and dragged her long, burgundy painted nail down his skin to the top of his briefs, feeling his muscles tighten under her touch. She hooked her finger under the elastic of his briefs and pulled downward, revealing the hard curve of his ass. Using both hands, she tugged the black underwear down his muscular thighs to the floor. He lifted his feet, one at a time, as she pulled the garment free and tossed it aside.

She avoided looking at his cock, wanting her anticipation to build. Trying not to think about the fact it would be hard and pulsing. Right now, his sexy ass was enough to keep her hormones hopping. She picked up the flogger she'd dropped to the floor and swished it lightly over his bare ass. Then she quivered the strands in a rippling motion up his back, giving him time to get used to the feel of the soft suede against his skin. Right now it would be like a gentle massage.

She drew back the flogger and flicked her wrist. The strands danced against his skin. Then she flicked again, striking his ass a little harder. She was rewarded by the sight of his butt clenching.

Her cell phone blipped, but she ignored it, gliding the suede over his tight ass again.

"Mistress, did you hear your phone? You just got a text."

She flicked the flogger again, striking him a slightly stinging blow.

"I'm not interested in texts right now."

"But... it might be important."

She pursed her lips. Had he planned something?

Reluctantly, she drew in a breath, then walked across the room and pulled her phone from her purse. Her gaze drifted to his cock. It stood tall and proud. Her heart thumped loudly. She had to will herself not to be distracted by her need to feel it inside her. She wanted to play out his punishment first, then she would allow herself to pay some attention to his stiff member.

She glanced at her phone.

Your safe word is Zebra. Say that word if you don't like how this unfolds.

Then another text appeared.

Respond yes if you want to play.

Both messages were from Abel's number.

What did he have planned? Anticipation quivered through her as she tapped in her response.

Yes.

Given Abel was standing in this room, with his hands chained behind his back, she assumed he'd used an app to send her a timed message. She had no idea what he had planned or why he had asked her for a response. Would that response trigger something to happen?

Ordinarily, she wouldn't allow a sub to take any kind of control like this, but this was outside their role playing, and she was delightfully curious.

She set down the phone and walked back to where Abel stood, gazing at his cock, which had deflated a little from its previous glory.

"Are you ready to continue your punishment?" she asked, her gaze lingering on his cock.

At her obvious attention, it stiffened again.

"Yes, Mistress."

She stepped behind him and flicked the strands across his back. Then she snapped the flogger harder.

As she pulled it back for another strike, she heard a click and the door flung open. Her eyes widened as two identical copies of Abel burst into the room.

"What are you doing to our brother?" one demanded.

Thrown off balance by the sight of the two large, muscular men heading her way, she stepped back. It was an incredibly bizarre experience seeing two men who looked exactly like the man she loved, especially with them striding toward her, glowering expressions on their faces.

But she quickly recovered her wits and stood tall. They were play acting, she was sure. In fact, it had probably been one of them who had sent the text giving her a safe word. She stopped her lips from quirking up in a smile. So they wanted to play, too.

This was certainly a crazy way to meet Abel's brothers for the first time.

"I'm giving him the punishment he deserves." She sent them a challenging stare.

"No one hurts our brother if we can help it," the left one said.

They each grabbed one of her arms and propelled her backwards. She found herself dumped onto one of the wooden dining room chairs. One brother held her arms behind her back while the other walked to the pole, then pulled a key from his pocket and unlocked the handcuffs. Abel and his brother strode toward her, Abel's big cock still standing straight up.

"Should we spank her?" the brother behind her asked.

"I'd love to spank that sexy round ass of hers," the brother beside Abel said, his eyes glittering.

She suddenly realized that the harness left her ass totally exposed. The thought of their big hands smacking her exposed flesh sent shivers of excitement through her.

"I don't know," Abel said, wrapping his hand around his cock. "I can think of other *punishments* we could inflict upon her."

He stepped close to her, his big cockhead an inch from her mouth. The man behind her curved his fingers around her head and pressed her forward until her lips touched Abel's cock.

"Open," he commanded.

Part of her panicked at losing control so completely, but she enjoyed the switch. It was exciting to be overpowered by these three powerful men. Men whom she instantly trusted, because she trusted Abel.

And going along with this scenario showed Abel that she was flexible and would succumb to his wishes, as long as they found a balance between their needs.

She obeyed and opened her mouth. Abel eased forward, sliding his big cock into her. She had to stretch to accommodate the plum-sized head. Her tongue swirled around him. He pushed deeper while the man behind her held her head firmly. Abel drew back, then glided forward again.

"Man, that is hot," the brother in front of her said. "I think we should all fill her sweet little mouth."

"Craig, hand me the cuffs," the brother behind her said as Abel drew back.

She immediately missed his hot, hard flesh in her mouth.

With Craig and Abel in front of her, she knew it was Drake behind her. He took the cuffs Craig handed him and she felt the cold bite of steel around one wrist, then the other. She tugged and found he'd fastened the cuffs around one of the slats on the back of the chair.

Drake stepped in front of her, too. Craig was already

dropping his pants to the floor as Drake unfastened his belt. She watched him pull back the leather, then release the buckle. His jeans landed on the floor with a *thunk*. Hungrily, she watched him bring out his big cock, then he stepped forward.

"Open," Drake said again.

She opened and he pushed his cock against her lips. The feel of this stranger's erection pushing into her mouth sent her insides fluttering. She'd never been with more than one man at a time and found it exhilarating. She wrapped her lips around him and squeezed as he slid further inside.

"She can take it deep," Abel said, his gaze locked on her lips surrounding his brother's cock.

Drake surged deeper and she relaxed her throat, allowing him access.

"Fuck, you're right." Then Drake drew back.

Craig stepped forward, his cock in his hand. "Don't forget about me."

He pressed his cock to her cheek and Drake pulled out. Craig immediately took his place, sliding inside her. God, she could feel the wetness pooling between her legs at being used by these three sexy men.

Craig thrust a couple of times, then pulled out and Abel slid inside. Each man thrust into her mouth several times, then pulled out to let the next brother fill her. They were all getting close and finally, when Craig pressed his cock to her lips, she turned her head, refusing to open her mouth. She did not want them to come yet.

"So you've decided to be uncooperative," Abel said.

He reached for her breast, but rather than cupping it like she thought he'd do, he grasped the fabric and tugged. The fabric ripped away from the side with a tearing sound and she realized it was held on by Velcro. Craig reached for her other breast and tore away that strip of fabric, too.

Suddenly, both men leaned forward and their lips surrounded her nipples, which swelled inside their hot, moist mouths.

Abel's hand slid around to her back, then he drew her forward. She arched toward them at the pressure, her breast thrusting deeper into their mouths. She heard another tearing sound and felt cool air against her slick, intimate folds, immediately followed by a hot mouth.

She arched her pelvis forward as Drake licked her wet slit. She moaned. The intense pleasure from the attention of three hot male mouths was overwhelming. She rocked her pelvis as Drake covered her clit and began to suck lightly. Her head fell back, draped over the back of the chair, as she rode the triple sensations of pure pleasure. As Drake's tongue teased her sensitive bud, his big fingers stroked over her slick flesh, then one slid inside her. She stifled a whimper. Another slipped inside and he thrust rhythmically, driving her pleasure higher. Craig sucked on her nipple and a moan escaped her lips.

"She's going to come," Abel said.

She opened her eyes to see him gazing at her with a smile. Craig sucked hard on her nipple as Drake kept thrusting into her. She arched against Drake's hand, wanting his fingers deeper, wishing it was a big, hard cock inside her. Then Drake drove deep at the same time as he sucked her clit and pleasure burst through her. While Abel watched her intently, she gasped, then wailed her release. She rode the wave of wild sensations, catapulting to sheer ecstasy.

Drake's fingers stilled and all the mouths eased away from her. She collapsed in the chair, sucking in air. The wooden back dug into her neck, but she didn't care.

Finally, she sat up straight. "Release me immediately," she said in her most commanding tone.

Drake's eyebrow quirked up. "And why should we do that?"

"Because I am in charge here." She locked gazes with Drake. "And you want to be dominated by me." She smiled. "You want to know what I will demand of you."

She widened her legs, watching their gazes drop to her slick, naked pussy.

"And how I will reward you."

Drake shifted his gaze back to hers, a glint of challenge in his blue eyes. But he stepped behind her and released the cuffs.

She stood up tall, a stern expression on her face, despite the fact she was basically naked.

"Now you all deserve to be punished." She placed her hands on her hips. "Abel."

"Yes, Mistress."

She was intensely aware of all three hot male gazes on her body.

"Fetch the riding crop."

"Yes, Ma'am." Abel walked to the drawer, then returned and handed her the crop.

She took it and ran her fingers along the thin, black rod. "Now the three of you will finish stripping, then lean over the back of the couch so I can see your tight, naked asses."

Abel, who was already naked walked to the back of the couch while the other two shed the rest of their clothes. A moment later, the three of them stood at the couch.

"Turn around and lean over," she instructed.

In unison, they turned, then rested their hands on the back of the couch and leaned forward. Her heart stammered at the sight of three such fine pairs of buttocks lined up in front of her. Abel was on the far left, then Craig—she thought it was Craig—which put Drake on the far right.

She walked behind them and stroked Abel's behind with

the side of the crop, then she ran it along Craig's ass, then Drake's.

She felt mischievous and more bold than usual, given the fact they'd just taken charge of her. She lifted the crop and slapped it across Craig's ass, resulting in a loud snapping sound. He flinched and a red heart—the shape of the leather tab on the end of the crop—formed on his skin. When she stroked the tip over Abel, he tensed. She drew back the crop, but smacked it across Drake's butt. Rewarded with another red heart, she turned back to Abel and flicked the crop across his as yet unblemished skin.

She stood admiring her handiwork. A delightful red heart on all three tight asses.

"Now you may thank me for your punishment."

"Thank you, Mistress," they all murmured.

She smacked all three of them in quick succession.

"I want more enthusiasm."

"Thank you, Mistress," they said with more gusto.

"Good." She stepped closer to their big bodies and stroked her fingertips over the red mark on Drake's ass. "You have a delightful heart on your ass."

She outlined it, then ran her fingers downward and cupped his balls. He widened his legs, giving her freer access. She fondled him, then shifted to Craig, running her hand over his mark. This time she stroked her hands around his hips to the front of him and found his cock. She leaned close to his body, pressing her bare breasts against his back and wrapped both hands around his swollen cock.

"Mmm. You're so big." She stroked him a couple of times, then turned to Abel. She especially longed to hold him in her hands. She cupped his butt and squeezed, as she reached around to grasp his cock with her other hand. She stroked his shaft, gliding her other hand down to caress his balls.

Reluctantly, she released him and stepped back. "You're

all so big and hard. I think it's time to put those big tools of yours to work. All of you stand up."

They stood and turned to face her. Their three long hard cocks stood at full attention.

"Drake, I'm sure there's some lube around here somewhere. Go and get it."

"Yes, Ma'am," he responded, then walked toward the bedroom.

"Abel, you sit on the couch."

As Abel sat down, Drake returned and handed her a tube. She opened it as she knelt in front of Abel, then she squeezed a generous amount of gel on his cock, then smoothed it over the head and shaft until it glistened. Then she stood and knelt on the couch beside him.

"Abel, I want you to push that big cock of yours into my ass." The very thought of it sent heat washing through her.

"Yes, Mistress." His words glowed with enthusiasm.

He stood up and moved behind her. Her breath caught when she felt his hot cockhead nudge against her back opening. She pushed her muscles as he pressed forward, sinking his cockhead into her tight channel. Oh, God, it felt so good as his big member slowly eased into her, stretching her wide.

She drew in a slow breath as he continued deeper until he finally filled her completely.

"Now sit," she said.

He grasped her hips and turned them both around, then sank onto the couch, taking her with him. Now she sat on his lap, her legs spread wide, facing the other two men.

"Do you like seeing me here with your brother's cock in my ass?" she asked.

They both affirmed, Drake addressing her as "Mistress" and Craig as "Ma'am."

She rocked a little on Abel's pelvis, shifting his cock

inside her, sending heat thrumming through her. He moaned a little and his brothers watched avidly.

"I give you both permission to touch me however you want."

Both men surged forward. Drake knelt down and stroked her breast, then licked her nipple before swallowing it into his hot mouth. Craig knelt between her knees and stroked her inner thighs. Quivers danced along her flesh at his light touch. Then he leaned forward and licked her slit.

"Oh, yes. I like that," she murmured.

Craig nuzzled her clean-shaven pussy, then teased her clit with his tongue. Drake slid his hand under Craig's mouth and pushed two big fingers inside her.

"Mistress, you're really wet," Drake said with a smile. "Would you like my hard cock inside your pussy?"

His fingers stroked her inner passage and she squeezed them inside her, longing for me.

"Oh, yes."

Craig shifted out of the way, his hand moving to his hard shaft as Drake positioned himself between her legs and pressed his cock to her wet opening.

"Yes. Drive your big cock inside me."

He thrust forward, filling her in one stroke. It was so tight with Abel's cock in her ass and Drake's in her pussy. She groaned, wanting more.

She grasped Drake's shoulders. "Deeper," she insisted.

He thrust forward, pushing further inside.

"Oh, God, yes. Now fuck me hard."

Both men pivoted their hips, gliding their cocks in and out. She sucked in a breath as intense sensations blasted through her. Behind Drake, Craig pumped his cock. During the haze of pleasure, she reached for him and he stepped close. She grasped his cock and squeezed, then began to pump in rhythm with the pumping of the two cocks inside her. A surge of joy flared through her.

"Oh, God, I'm going to come," she said.

Abel and Drake pumped faster, Drake pushing deeper and harder. She gasped as her insides swelled with bliss, then a mind-shattering orgasm exploded within her.

Still they pumped. Drake thrust deep and ground against her, then hot liquid filled her. Behind her, Abel groaned and twitched inside her.

Craig tapped Drake's shoulder and Drake's cock slipped from her as he moved aside. Immediately, Craig's engorged cock thrust deep inside her. She groaned, as spectacular pleasure blasted through her again and he erupted inside her. The hardness of him, and the feel of his cock pulsing inside her catapulted her over the edge again. Her quiet moans turned to a wail as Craig continued to pump into her, until she finally collapsed against Abel, totally spent.

Abel's cock had deflated after he'd come, but it twitched inside her with new life. She rested her head against his shoulder and gazed up at him.

"Really? You want to go again?"

He laughed. "Well, only if my Mistress allows it."

She smiled. "Maybe later. Right now I need to catch my breath."

Suddenly, she felt the world tilt around her as Abel lifted and rolled her onto her back on the couch, then prowled over her, trapping her beneath his big body. He smiled, then captured her lips. His mouth moved on hers passionately and she wrapped her arms around him, so glad to be in his embrace once more.

When he released her lips, she gazed up at him.

"So does this mean you're okay with me being a Domme?"

"Are you kidding? I find it sexy as hell." He grinned. "Especially the way you kept my brothers in line."

She laughed as he sat up, pulling her onto his lap.

"By the way, meet Drake and Craig," he said.

She held out her hand and each brother shook it with a warm squeeze. "It's a pleasure to finally meet you."

"I think pleasure is an understatement," Craig said. "This whole thing was fucking hot."

She giggled in total agreement. "I hope we can do it again."

"Fuck yeah," Craig said. "We'll be at your beck and call."

Happily, she rested her head against Abel's chest. He kissed the top of her head, then cleared his throat.

"Uh, you do realize that if we continue to share that means... well..." He gazed at her uncertainly.

"What our brother is trying to point out is that Drake and I are married, and our wives like being shared, too."

"Oh." She gazed at Abel. "That means you'll be having sex with their wives, too."

Abel shrugged. "It's only fair. Are you okay with that?"

She had hoped to have a long term, committed relationship with Abel. The thought of him having sex with other women was unsettling, but she couldn't expect his brothers to share her—and after this evening, she knew she wanted the sharing to continue—if she wasn't willing to share him in return.

He leaned in to murmur in her ear. "Because if you're not, I'll stop. Being with you is more important to me than anything. I love you."

Her heart swelled with joy at hearing those words. She threw her arms around him and kissed him with all the passion burning inside her.

"As long as you love me, we'll find a way to make it work."

She smiled. "I loved being with all three of you. I'm sure I can get used to you... uh... entertaining their wives."

"You know, you don't have to be left out of it," Drake said. "The three of us have been with both Marie and Lori."

She glanced at him in surprise. "So the sharing could be... broader?"

Craig smiled. "I think both our wives would love to learn a thing or two from you."

"To keep you two in line, you mean?" she asked with a smile.

"Maybe, but I mean I think they'd love to be dominated by you, too. I know Lori has a thing for handcuffs."

Heat swirled through her at the thought of two women under her control. Ideas started popping through her head about how she could command them to give and receive pleasure with the three men... and herself. That last thought surprised her, but now images of soft, feminine hands stroking her, female mouths licking and caressing her body... sent desire pulsing through her.

"You know," she said, "I think I might be ready to do a little sharing again right now."

Abel laughed. "Hold that thought, because I definitely like that idea, but first, I have one more secret."

"Oh, no. After what we've already revealed, I'm afraid to ask what it is," she said.

"Then don't ask, just listen." Then Abel sank to his knees in front of her.

"What's going on?" she asked.

His brothers moved around the room, but her gaze remained locked on Abel's dark, serious eyes.

"I'm not much for speeches or poetry," he said. "All I want to say is that I love you deeply and I want to spend the rest of my life with you."

Drake handed Abel something and he held it out. It was a

brown velvet box, which he snapped open. Inside was a beautiful, shimmering solitaire diamond ring.

"Will you marry me?"

Joy soared within her and she threw her arms around him. "Yes! Of course, I will!"

He hugged her tight, crushing her against his muscular body, but she didn't mind. She had dreamed of them being together and now that would be a reality.

As soon as he released her lips, Drake dragged her to her feet and into a bear hug. God, here she was in her soon-to-be brother-in-law's arms and they were both naked, her soft breasts crushed against his hard chest. And from the feel of things, that's not the only thing that was hard right now.

Craig spun her away from Drake and hugged her tight, too. "Welcome to the family."

She laughed. "You are a friendly bunch."

Abel laughed as he stood up and pulled her back into his arms again. "And we're about to get a whole lot friendlier."

AFTERWORD

*I hope you enjoyed **Three Happy Endings**.*

If you did, please post a review at your favorite online store because that's the best way to help me write more stories like this.

If not, please email me at <u>Opal@OpalCarew.com</u> because I love to hear from my wonderful readers.

FREE EBOOKS

Would you like more hot, sexy stories?
Join the Opal Carew Reader Group
to receive free erotic reads!

Just go to
OpalCarew.com/ReaderGroup

Patreon.com/OpalCarew

EXCERPTS

If you liked the THREE series, you will almost certainly like Opal's other short erotica stories, such her **Red Hot Fantasies** series.

If you'd like something equally hot, but novel length, you will definitely enjoy Opal's poignant erotic romance novel, **Dirty Talk,** winner of both the **2018 Golden Leaf** and **2018 Golden Quill** awards. It's about about a woman struggling with her sexuality because of a devastating trauma from her past, and the strong, sensitive man who helps her find her way.

Moving more toward erotica, Opal writes under the pseudonym Ruby Carew, and two recommendations include her **All He Wants Christmas Collection**, which asks *"What happens when you storm out of the jerk's apartment on a cold winter night wearing next to nothing?"*, and her **Stacy** series, which asks *"What would you do when the older man you've always had a crush on is the only one you can turn to?"*.

All of the above stories can be found at **OpalCarew.com** or **RubyCarew.com**

Here is an excerpt for the **Dirty Talk** series…

DIRTY TALK, BOOKS 1 & 2

OPAL CAREW

Opal Carew's **Dirty Talk** series is a poignant erotic romance about a woman struggling with her sexuality because of a devastating trauma from her past, and the strong, sensitive man who helps her find her way. If you love bad-assed alpha heroes with a strong, protective streak then you'll love **Dirty Talk**!

Sonny has a debilitating fear of men. Tal is a scary looking tattooed bad-ass. Can Tal get Sonny past her fear and help her become whole?

Sonny longs to feel the intimate touch of a man. But she is haunted by a past trauma that leaves her terrified of being with a man. Even when she dreams of being in a man's arms, the steamy sexual situation turns into a nightmare.

Sonny has found one way to cope. A stranger's voice has been her salvation.

Tal wants a woman to love him. To have a real, long-lasting relationship. But most women are intimidated by his bad-ass appearance, with his tattoos, piercings, and broad, muscular frame.

Tal looks the way he does because of a past fraught with pain. The tattoos aren't going anywhere, so he needs to find a woman who will accept him for who he is... and was.

When Tal sees Sonny, he senses in her a kindred spirit. The haunting pain in her eyes draws him, but he flinches every time fear flickers across her face when she sees him.

Can Tal find a way to break through Sonny's barriers and start something that might heal them both?

Dirty Talk, Books 1 & 2 is a collection of the first two exciting episodes in Opal Carew's Dirty Talk series. If you love erotic romance with a poignant story, a deeply wounded alpha hero who will do anything to protect his woman, and a heroine struggling to accept love, then this is the series for you!

Buy this collection today to enjoy this poignant, erotic romance story!

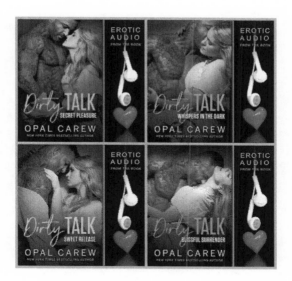

Erotic Audios

In this collection, Sonny listens to erotic audios that Tal makes for her. These are also available for you to buy. For more information go to **OpalCarew.com/DirtyTalk**

Be sure to listen to them alone--or with your lover—and be ready for your panties to melt right off!

Excerpt

Sonny sighed, enjoying the heat of the sunshine on her back. Warm and relaxing. Soothing her tension.

Last night had been difficult for her. To others, it seemed like she easily walked away from any man, totally unaffected. But the truth was, her date with Bryan had been hard on her. As much as she would never consider going out with him, it wasn't really because she didn't want to. She just... couldn't.

Deep down inside, though, she longed for a loving relationship with a man. To meet someone, go out on a date. To build a loving connection.

To be *touched* by a man.

Oh, God, she wanted that so much. But she was too afraid.

Anytime her natural urges bubbled to the surface, like they had last night with Bryan, it wasn't long before she started having dreams. Those dreams started off sweet and loving, then turned hot and steamy, searing her senses. Inevitably, however, they turned dark and terrifying and she'd wake up shaking, her whole body sweating.

If only she could just have nice, steamy sex dreams that helped her relieve her ache.

Her skin prickled and a heated awareness washed through her body, but it wasn't from thoughts of having a nice sexual fantasy.

Someone was watching her.

She suddenly became very conscious of her situation. Wearing just a bikini. Her top undone.

Alone on the roof of the building.

She drew in a deep breath.

It was the middle of a sunny summer afternoon on a Thursday. Usually no one came up to the pool this time of day. Anyone who wanted to enjoy the warm afternoon and go in the water normally went to the beach a few blocks away.

But someone was definitely watching her and it must be from inside, because she would have heard the sliding glass doors open.

She sucked in a breath of air, calming herself. It had taken her a long time to build up her courage to make these outings to the pool and she wasn't going to let herself slide back to the blinding fear. There were security cameras on the deck and she was in view of one right now. She always let Leandra know when she was going to sun herself on the deck, just with a casual message, as part of letting her know how her day was going.

If anything happened, it would be on the security film. Not that she'd let it get that far if she could help it. She wasn't powerless. She had pepper spray in her bag, her cell phone handy so she could quickly dial 911, and she'd taken self-defense classes.

She reached around and fastened her bikini top, then slowly sat up. Casually, she reached for her silky, black floral cover up and pulled it on, carefully not looking toward the windows. She wanted to be covered and feeling a little more settled when she faced the intruder.

Before she had a chance, though, the sliding doors opened. She glanced up to see a man step onto the deck.

She sighed in relief when she saw it was Steve from the tenth floor. They had mutual friends in the building and had gotten to know each other and become friends of sorts.

He was a really nice guy. And good looking, with his broad shoulders, well-defined torso, and dark blond hair swept back from his handsome face.

Steve glanced over his shoulder at the open door. It seemed he was waiting for someone to join him.

When his gaze swept outside again, he saw her for the first time.

His face beamed with his warm, friendly smile. "Hi, Sonny. Nice afternoon."

"Yes, it is."

She wouldn't mind chatting with him. She'd found she was always pretty comfortable around Steve which was nice for a change, but she didn't know how to give out an inviting vibe.

She pulled her bag closer, and routed through it, just for something to distract herself.

Then another man stepped outside.

She glanced up and her heart thumped to life.

The man was...breathtaking.

His body was big and powerful. His arms and chest bulged with muscles and he had tattoos covering his body. She couldn't tell what they all were since they were so dense, but she did make out a thorny rose vine coiling along one arm and around his torso, tendrils even coiling up his neck.

His hair was dark brown, shaved close to his head, and his ear glinted with piercings.

He glanced at her and smiled. Immediately, she dropped her gaze to her bag and she started sorting through it again, as if looking for something.

They started to walk and she was afraid they'd come over, but instead they headed toward some chairs closer to the edge of the deck.

Oh, God, the man was so heart-stoppingly masculine. Her body tingled as her hormones sparked to life.

Which she didn't understand. She should be afraid, but the sensation pulsing through her was pure, unadulterated lust.

Unnerved, she grabbed her book and suntan lotion and shoved them into her bag, then pushed her towel in, too. She slipped on her sandals and surged to her feet, then hurried to the door. As she slid it open, she glanced over her shoulder and saw that the big man was watching her, a frown on his face.

Did he think she was running away from him?

She didn't want any man to think she was afraid of him—showing strength was important—but right now, the threat she faced was her own unbridled libido. She didn't understand her reaction to him and that unsettled her so much she had to escape.

She closed the door behind her and hurried away.

* * *

Tal watched the woman practically run off, his stomach clenching. All he'd done was smile at her. He hadn't said a word. Hadn't made a move toward her. Yet she'd up and fled.

He would have liked to have talked to her. Gotten to know her a little. There was something about her.

She was a beautiful woman, with her long, blonde hair cascading in waves over her shoulders. A pretty face with kissable heart-shaped lips. And he'd caught more than a glimpse of her curvy body through the glass when she'd sat up to pull on her cover up.

But what attracted him was more than that.

There was an aura of vulnerability around her. And a sadness in her eyes.

He sensed a need in her to have someone or something more in her life.

Or maybe he was just reflecting his own feelings onto her.

It caused him real pain that she would take one look at him and run away, as if he were some kind of threat.

"She's pretty, right?" Steve said.

"Yes, she is." He glanced at his friend. "Are you interested in her?"

"Well, yeah, what man wouldn't be? But I don't think we'd work out. We've talked a few times—she's friends with my friend Meghan—but we seem to be developing more of a casual rapport rather than a romantic relationship. If you want to pursue her, don't worry about me."

"I might if she didn't seem so terrified of me."

"Hey, if you're interested, don't give up on her too fast. I think she's been through something. She has these haunted eyes, you know? But I'm sure she's trying to work through it. She'd need someone who's willing to be patient and slow." He shrugged. "But I think she'd be worth it."

Tal glanced at the door she'd escaped through.

"Yeah, I think maybe you're right."

~

ALSO BY OPAL CAREW

Legend

🥇 🥇 🥇 - Contest Win

🎗 - Contest Finalist

🖼 - Sexiest Cover Win

Contemporary erotic short stories and novellas

Taken by Storm

(prequel to His to Possess)

Debt of Honor 🥇

Dirty Talk series 🥇 🥇 🎗

Dirty Talk, Secret Pleasure

Dirty Talk, Whispers in the Dark

Dirty Talk, Sweet Release

Dirty Talk, Blissful Surrender

Mastered By series

Played by the Master

Mastered by the Boss

Mastered by my Guardian

Mastered by the CEO 🥇 🖼

Mastered by her Captor

Mastered by the Sheikh

The Office Slave series

∾

Futuristic erotic romance novellas

Slaves of Love

Abducted series

(formerly Celestial Soul-Mates series)

Forbidden Mate

Unwilling Mate

Rebel Mate

Illicit Mate

Captive Mate

∼

Fantasy erotic romance

Crystal Genie

∼

Collections and Anthologies

Submitting to His Rules

Mastered by the Boss

Mastered by the CEO

Surrendering to His Rules

Mastered by her Captor

Mastered by the Sheikh

Owned by the Sheikh

Mastered by the Sheikh

Debt of Honor

Slaves of Love

Total Surrender

Played by the Master

The Office Slave

Three

Dirty Talk, Books 1 & 2
Dirty Talk, Books 3 & 4
Dirty Talk, The Complete Series

The Office Slave Series, Book 1 & 2

The Office Slave Series, Book 3 & 4

The Office Slave Series, Book 5 & 6

The Office Slave Series, Book 7 & Bonus

Red Hot Fantasies, Volume 1 (Books 1-3)

Red Hot Fantasies, Volume 2 (Books 4-5)

Ready to Ride, Book 1 & 2

Three Happy Endings (Books 1-3)

Turn Up The Heat (anthology)

Slaves of Love

Northern Heat (anthology)

Three

~

Contemporary erotic romance novels

Stroke of Luck

X Marks the Spot

Heat 🧍 🧍 ⬛

A Fare To Remember

Nailed 🧍 ⬛

My Best Friend's Stepfather 🧍

Stepbrother, Mine 🧍

Hard Ride 🔔 🔔

Riding Steele 🧍

His To Claim 🧍

His To Possess 🧍

His To Command 🔔

Illicit

Insatiable 🔔

Secret Weapon

Total Abandon ⬛

Pleasure Bound 🔔 🧍 🧍

Bliss 🔔 🧍 🧍

Forbidden Heat 🔔 🧍

Secret Ties 🔔 🧍 🧍

Six 🧍 🧍

Blush 🔔 🧍 🧍 ⬛

Swing 🔔 🧍 🧍

Twin Fantasies 🧍 🧍

Contemporary erotic romance (ebook only)

Meat

Big Package

Drilled

ALSO BY RUBY CAREW

ALSO BY AMBER CAREW

Romance Novels

Contemporary

In Too Deep

The Cinderella Obsession

Virgin Wanted

Fantasy

Christmas Angel

I Dream of Genie

Spellbound

Futuristic

Virtual Love

ABOUT THE AUTHOR

Opal Carew is a *New York Times* and *USA Today* bestselling author of poignant contemporary and sci-fi romance. Her books have won several awards, including the National Readers' Choice Award (twice), the Golden Leaf Award (3 times), the Golden Quill (4 times), the CRA Award of Excellence, and Silken Sands.

Opal writes about passion, love, and taking risks. Her heroines follow their hearts and push past the fear that stops them from realizing their dreams... to the excitement and love of happily-ever-after.

Opal loves nail polish, cats, crystals, dragons, feathers, pink hair, the occult, Manga artwork, Zentangle, and all that glitters. She grew up in Toronto, and now lives in Ottawa with her husband, huge nail polish collection, and five cats.

One of her sons just finished his second Masters degree in Geopolitics (first at Sussex University in the UK and second at Carleton University in Ottawa.) The other son is doing his Masters at the University of Toronto. Yes, mom is proud!

Social Media Links

Reader Group: OpalCarew.com/ReaderGroup
Patreon: OpalCarew
Website: OpalCarew.com

Facebook: OpalCarewRomanceAuthor
Twitter: @OpalCarew
Pinterest: opalcarew
Goodreads: bit.ly/OC_Goodreads
Contact Opal: bit.ly/contactopal